The Magical Animal
ADOPTION AGENCY
3 THE MISSING MAGIC

BY **Kallie George**

ILLUSTRATED BY
Alexandra Boiger

HARPERCOLLINS PUBLISHERS LTD

ALSO BY KALLIE GEORGE

The Magical Animal Adoption Agency, Book 1: Clover's Luck
The Magical Animal Adoption Agency, Book 2: The Enchanted Egg

To T and Marie
—K.G.

To you, dear Reader
—A.B.

The Missing Magic
Text copyright © 2016 by Kallie George.
Illustrations copyright © 2016 by Alexandra Boiger.
All rights reserved.

Published by HarperCollins Publishers Ltd

First Canadian Edition

HarperCollins books may be purchased for educational, business, or sales
promotional use through our Special Markets Department.

HarperCollins Publishers Ltd
2 Bloor Street East, 20th Floor
Toronto, Ontario, Canada
M4W 1A8

www.harpercollins.ca

Library and Archives Canada Cataloguing in Publication
information is available upon request

ISBN 978-1-44341-986-4

Printed and bound in the United States
RRD 9 8 7 6 5 4 3 2 1

Contents

1
Oliver the "Expert"

Sweet things are for sharing. Picture postcards. Cozy cuddles. Cupcakes so fluffy they float.

Over the summer, Clover had shared all of these: postcards with her friend Emma, who was away at Pony Camp; cuddles with Dipity, her green kitten; and cupcakes at a picnic with leprechauns, giants, and a ghost.

But the sweetest thing in Clover's life couldn't be shared with anyone—well, anyone non-magical, that is. It was the secret of the Magical Animal Adoption Agency, hidden in the Woods and filled with unicorns, fairy horses, and even an invisible flying puppy!

Mr. Jams had entrusted her with the secret. He owned the Agency and had hired her as a volunteer at the start of the summer. Mr. Jams said that often-times non-magical people didn't know how to deal with magic, and so that was why Clover couldn't write to Emma about it or tell her parents. They knew that she was working at an animal adoption agency, and that was it. Sometimes she wished she could tell them. Mostly she was happy enough to keep the secret to herself.

Now, however, there was someone she had no choice but to share the Agency with—and having him around was anything but sweet.

Oliver Von Hoof was a magical animal expert. He had written the volume on enchanted eggs in the *Magical Animal Encyclopedia*, as well as two other volumes, even though he was only slightly older than Clover. Mr. Jams had invited him to examine a giant  spotted egg at the Agency, but it had hatched before he arrived. Inside was Picnic, the invisible puppy. Mr. Jams had insisted Oliver stay, so he could observe the puppy and work on a new book about invisible animals.

"Plus he'll be able to lend a hand," Mr. Jams had added.

So far, though, he wasn't helping at all.

Clover and Oliver were in the tack room, where the stables' supplies were kept, getting ready to start a new task. Mr. Jams had asked them to polish the unicorns' horns while he minded the front desk.

"Can you pass me a bottle of stardust?" Clover asked. "And one bottle of moonbeams? Mr. Jams said we have to mix them together to make the polish."

Oliver wasn't listening. He was scribbling words in his notebook. "Out-of-sight canines are usually winged. . . ." He paused. "Hmm . . . 'out-of-sight' is not right, is it? I suppose I could use 'invisible' again, but I've used it fifty-seven times in the first chapter alone."

"Oliver, the stardust and moonbeams!" prompted Clover.

Oliver set down his notebook and pushed his glasses up his nose. "Did you say something?"

"Ugh," groaned Clover, getting the ingredients herself.

The stardust was easy to spot, twinkling brightly on the shelf just above the bridles.

The bottles of moonbeams, however, were harder to find, packed away in a dusty box. They glowed in

3

varying degrees that matched their labels—from bright FULL MOON to pale CRESCENT.

One bottle shone with a slightly blue tinge, like a pool of clear water. BLUE MOON, its label read. Clover had never heard of a blue moon before. "Is that even a real thing?"

"Why, of course," said Oliver, who was now peering over her shoulder. "It is the second full moon in a single month, which is rare but predictable, if you are able to do the calculations, of course."

"Oh," said Clover. She wondered how the beams were collected. Oliver probably knew, but she didn't want another lecture.

So, instead of asking, she took a bottle of crescent moonbeams, which was the type Mr. Jams said they needed, from the box. Then she found a spoon and wooden bowl, crusted with sparkles, for mixing the polish. The cork on the stardust was stuck in tight. But Oliver was writing again and was too absorbed to notice her struggling with it.

Before Clover could remind him that he was *supposed* to be helping her, the bell in the front room rang.

"Package here!" came the friendly voice of Cedric, the delivery-man (well, delivery-centaur, to be specific). "Package for Oliver Von Hoof!"

"I guess Mr. Jams has stepped away from the front desk," Oliver said, pushing his glasses up his nose. "I'd better go get the package. It *is* for me." He gathered his notebook and quill. "I wonder what it could be."

"But . . ." started Clover, still trying to remove the cork, "what about . . . ?"

"Don't fret. I'll return soon." And with that, Oliver was gone.

Clover couldn't believe it. He had gotten out of helping *again*. Yesterday had been the same. They were supposed to clean the big tank to prepare for the arrival of a hippocampus, a half-horse, half-fish creature. But just at the hard part—pouring the water in—he disappeared because he remembered a vital fact he *had* to add to his book. And he hadn't returned. *This time he'd better*, thought Clover. She tugged at the cork.

POOF!

Out it came—and a cloud of stardust billowed out too, covering her dress.

She sighed as she brushed it off as best she could.

Luckily, the cork on the moonbeams slipped free easily. As Clover stirred the two ingredients together, lumps of stardust melted, and so did her annoyance. After all, how many times had she wished upon stars that she could be with animals? And now here she was, working with *magical* animals—and actually touching bits of stars! She couldn't stay upset when she thought about that.

At last the polish was ready. With a rag and the bowl of paste in hand, Clover headed out of the tack room to begin the actual work.

However, polishing the first unicorn's horn proved impossible! Plum (or Sugar-plumsy-Wumsy, as he had been named by the princess who'd owned him) wouldn't lie down or stay still, and he kept trying to eat the rag. So instead of polishing his horn, Clover filled up his bucket with a generous helping of hearty oats and moved on to Sunny's stall.

Trying to polish Sunny's horn was impossible too. Sunny (or Smoochie-Coochie Sunshine) was an

especially small unicorn with long eyelashes. Supposedly the princess who had owned him had tried curling them and poked one of Sunny's eyes. The minute Clover brought the rag up to Sunny's horn, his left eye began to fill with tears. Whether it was from some stardust that got into it or out of fear, she didn't know. But she couldn't possibly polish his horn if it upset him so.

"There, there," she said, gently patting his nose until he calmed down.

Where is Oliver? Clover wondered. *He should be back by now.* Cedric liked to chat, but it shouldn't take *that* long to get mail from him.

With a sigh, she moved on to Tootsie.

Tootsie (or Tootise-Wootsie Wugums) was triple trouble! Her horn was ticklish, and every time Clover touched it with the rag, Tootsie shook it. On the third try, the horn missed Clover by inches, and she jumped back just in time. The bowl of polish slipped from her hands and landed upside down on the stall floor in a sparkly, gucky mess.

"Ugh!" cried Clover. "I can't do this by myself!" Oliver wasn't getting out of helping this time.

She scooped up as much of the polish as she could and set the bowl down outside the stall. After giving

Tootsie's nose a pat, she closed the stall gate. Then she stormed out of the stables and into the main hall of the Agency. She was about to call for Oliver when she heard voices coming from the small animals' room.

She could hear Oliver, Mr. Jams, and someone else too—a girl!

Oliver *was* helping. He was helping with an adoption!

2

Reckless with Relics

The door to the small animals' room was slightly ajar, and Clover peered in.

Mr. Jams, Oliver, and a girl around Clover's age stood in front of the magic kittens' cage. Mr. Jams had his back to the door, and Oliver and the girl were facing Clover, but they were busy talking and didn't seem to notice her.

The girl looked like a witch, with pointy boots and a dress patterned with bats and spiders. Her long black hair was streaked with purple and fell across one eye. She kept flicking it away with a toss of her head as she smiled up at Oliver and then down again at the kitten he was holding awkwardly in his arms.

"Now, Oliver, describe the kitten to the young lady," said Mr. Jams.

Clover felt a twinge of jealousy. Mr. Jams was teaching Oliver to do an adoption. Sure, Clover wanted Oliver to help out with the chores, but adoptions were different. They were *her* job, and she was good at them. She didn't need help with those.

"This feline has a unique and rare magical ability—ocular glaciation," said Oliver.

Ocular glaciation? Clover rolled her eyes. Why not just say the kitten shoots freeze rays?

But the young witch seemed impressed. "That's wicked!" she giggled, reaching out to pet Blizzard's tiny black head. "I've started a lemonade stand, and Blizzard could help me keep the cups chilled. Oh, Ollie, I think he's perfect! You don't mind if I call you Ollie, do you?"

"Oh, bother," Clover muttered under her breath.

She didn't want to overhear any more of this adoption. But she didn't want to go back to polishing horns either, at least not until she got some help.

Then she turned and saw the steps up to the tower. And she had an idea.

In all the weeks Clover had worked at the Agency, she'd never been up to the tower. She knew it was where Mr. Jams lived, and now Oliver too. But there were no animals there, and everything for the animals' care was on the main floor, so she'd never needed to go up. Plus Mr. Jams hadn't invited her. And it hadn't mattered. Now, somehow, it did.

If Oliver was receiving deliveries at the Agency, surely that meant he wasn't planning on leaving any time soon. *What was in the parcel?* she wondered. She had to know.

And so, after shaking off as much of the stardust from her dress as she could (she didn't want to leave a glittery trail), she began tiptoeing up the tower steps. Behind her, she heard a mew. It was Dipity, glaring up at her from the bottom of the stairs, as though he knew just what she was about to do.

Clover frowned. "Shoo," she told her kitten.

But Dipity didn't listen. Dipity *never* listened. Instead he sat there, his tail flicking.

So Clover kept going and was pleased when Dipity joined her on the steps, padding alongside. The staircase spiraled around and around, at last ending in a circular landing with a rug and three doors. Two of the doors were open.

The room to Clover's right was a bathroom, with toothbrushes sticking out of an empty jam jar, towels on the floor, and an old toaster instead of a mirror propped up in front of the sink, one of its shiny sides facing out.

The next was clearly Mr. Jams's room. It was a mess. Clover could see papers, books, and clothes piled everywhere. The only form of organization seemed to be empty jam jars—which held everything from socks and ties to butter knives and buckles. There were even things stuffed under the bed, including something that glinted. Clover bent down and saw it was a knight's helmet. This was the second object related to knights she'd found in the Agency. There was a sword in the front room too.

"Why does Mr. Jams have a helmet? And a sword?" wondered Clover aloud. "Do you know?" she asked Dipity.

But her kitten was gone. He had moved on to the

final room, and Clover did too, cautiously pushing its door open.

The room was filled with books—too many for Oliver to have brought here himself. There were some books downstairs, but nothing like this. *It must be Mr. Jams's private library*, thought Clover. In between the shelves, there was just enough space for a desk and a cot. But he wasn't just sleeping there; he had practically moved in! Eggs—or at least images of them—were everywhere.

Spotted eggs patterned the blanket on the tiny cot, and the pillow was shaped like an egg. Beside the cot was a desk with all the volumes of the *Magical Animal Encyclopedia*, a jar of wands, a pile of papers held down by an egg-shaped paperweight, and an inkwell that seemed to be made from an eggshell.

Dipity jumped onto the desk and began to play with a feather that was bookmarking one of the encyclopedias while Clover turned her attention to the box that had been delivered by Cedric. It was beside the desk, and marked SPECIAL DELIVERY! FRAGILE!

The box was open, but only the first item was unwrapped. Oliver must have just started looking through the contents when the witch arrived.

Clover picked up the first object.

It was a set of tiny antlers. FROM A PETRIFIED JACK-ALOPE, read its tag.

She had met a creature with antlers like these! Lulu the leprechaun had an invisible bunny with them. Oliver had examined it—by touch only, of course—before Lulu left on a family trip.

What else might I find? Clover wondered, pushing back some of the tissue paper.

Alongside the antlers, there was a giant fossilized footprint as big as a dragon's, a patch of fur that disappeared when it was held up to the light, a see-through scale from a "polo serpent," and, last but not least, a collar with a tag that said it belonged to a shadow-creature.

These must be relics from invisible animals, thought Clover, *to help Oliver with his book. But what's the point of him staying here if he needs everything sent to him?*

She was checking the box again, to make sure she hadn't missed anything, when something tucked in the bottom corner caught her eye. It was a glittering chain with a charm in the shape of a sun. It wasn't even wrapped. She took it out. Usually, Clover didn't care much for jewelry, but the chain felt good between her fingers, smooth and cool, and the sun charm was very pretty, like a piece of honey-colored glass.

16

Clover knew she should put it back, but she hesitated. Oliver probably wouldn't wear a necklace—especially one that wasn't egg-shaped. And it seemed like it was in the box by mistake. . . . *I'll just wear it for a moment*, she thought.

The chain was too small to go over her head, but there was a clasp, and it was easy to undo. The charm was smooth and cool against her skin. She liked wearing it. *I'll put it back last*, she thought, and she began repacking the relics.

Clover was almost done when she noticed a piece of paper that she had missed before, tucked in among the tissue. Her eyes read it before her heart told her not to.

Dear Oliver,

Mother told me of your interest in invisible animals. Does that mean you will be writing another one of your books? If so, I do hope this one is significantly shorter.

The museum was going to put this box of relics into storage, but, since I'm the curator and can do such things, I decided to send it to you instead. No need to thank me.

I hear you will be staying on at the MAAA.

Good luck with your interactions with the animals. Try not to get eaten.

Your brother,
Barnaby Von Hoof

P.S. Did you hear? I was recently awarded my sixth scholarship from the Royal Claw and Tooth Society!

Ugh! Oliver's brother sounded even more annoying than he was!

Clover tucked the letter back in the box. "Okay," she said to Dipity. "Time to go." She stood up. And then she remembered the necklace. Even if no one would miss it, it wasn't hers. She was about to take it off when . . .

"Go?" said a familiar voice behind her. It was Mr. Jams. "But what are you doing here, Clover?"

3

Sir Walter Windsmith

Clover's face burned. She quickly hid the charm under her dress, where the key to the Agency hung as well. Then she slowly turned around to face Mr. Jams and Oliver, who were standing in the doorway.

"I thought you were in the stables, polishing the horns?" Mr. Jams said, tugging at his beard.

"I was, but . . ." started Clover.

"Oh, hornswaggle!" said Mr. Jams, shaking his head and glancing at Oliver. "I had asked you *both* to do the job, hadn't I? I didn't mean to steal Oliver away, but an opportunity presented itself."

"I was doing an adoption," Oliver, beaming, told Clover. "And it went splendidly. Although I really do need to fix the mistakes on the forms. Two spelling errors."

Mr. Jams chuckled. "Come, come. I was going to find that balm for you. Ocular glaciation can cause a nasty burn."

"It's nothing, really," said Oliver, but Clover saw, with some satisfaction, a red patch on his hand. *She* wouldn't have gotten burned by Blizzard.

"Yes, well, a bit of Bettering Balm never hurt anyone," said Mr. Jams. "Clover, why don't you give Picnic a walk? He's bouncing all over the place. We can work on the horns together this afternoon."

✦

And so, moments later, Clover was trudging down the path that curved like a dragon's tail, with Picnic's collar floating ahead of her, his leash stretched tight like the string of a kite. Not far from the gate, she passed a fisherman pulling a large tank, but she barely noticed, lost in thought.

Clover knew she was good with the animals. Mr. Jams himself had said so. She belonged at the Agency. Though she hadn't given much thought to what might happen when school started, she hoped she could keep volunteering there after class and on weekends. But with Oliver doing adoptions, did Mr. Jams have other plans? She didn't know.

She *did* know that she shouldn't have snooped through Oliver's things. And she shouldn't have taken the necklace. Not that she meant to. *I'll put it back before anyone notices*, she thought, fiddling with the clasp with one hand. It wouldn't undo. She'd have to try again, properly, when she wasn't walking Picnic.

As they were nearing the fork in the path, Picnic's bell jingled.

He came swooping down—right into her arms, nearly toppling her over. "What's up?" she said, giving his wings a pat.

An answer came a moment later—in the form of a song.

It was low and sad, and sounded almost like musical sobbing. *Is it a bird?* she wondered.

As she turned the bend, the music-maker came into sight. It *was* a bird, perched on the sign that said HEART on the big tree at the crossroads. This was no ordinary bird, however. It was magical. It had to be, because what other bird could look like it was on fire? Its eyes smoldered, its feathers blazed red and gold like flames, and the tips of its wings and tail looked burnt. In fact, bits of them were crumbling and drifting down like ash, landing at the feet of . . . a knight.

At least, Clover thought he might be a knight because of his silver helmet and the sword hanging from his belt. But she wasn't sure. He was tall and thin,

like the branch of a willow tree, with arms no bigger around than hers. It was hard to imagine him swinging a sword. And his voice, too, was certainly not what she expected from a knight (at least not the knights Mr. Jams often complained about, intent on dragon-head trophies). This knight was speaking in verse:

> *"Dear Phoebe, dear pet,*
> *Fly down, fly to me,*
> *Soon we'll be there,*
> *For . . . a nice cup of tea . . .*

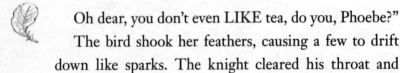

Oh dear, you don't even LIKE tea, do you, Phoebe?"

The bird shook her feathers, causing a few to drift down like sparks. The knight cleared his throat and tried again:

> *"Dear Phoebe, my friend,*
> *It's just round the bend,*
> *It's a place you can rest*
> *And build a fine nest . . ."*

He looked up at the bird hopefully. "That's better, right?"

But the bird clacked her beak and then continued her own song. The knight threw his hands up in the air in frustration.

"Excuse me," said Clover.

The knight turned. The visor of his helmet was up. His eyes were light blue, like the sky, but with dark circles under them, as though he hadn't slept for days. His smile, however, was kind and genuine. "Oh, hello. I don't suppose you have any fire berries?"

Clover shook her head. "There might be some at the Agency, though."

"The Agency? The Magical Animal Adoption Agency? That's just where we're headed. At least, so I hope. Alas, I have never yet managed to visit." The knight took another look at Clover. Then he whistled. "You must be Clover. Sir—I mean, *Mr.*—Jams called me when you first arrived. Why, he said . . . No . . . only rhyme will do. . . ." The knight cleared his throat:

> *"A gentle hand,*
> *To care and tend,*
> *A plucky heart,*
> *She's animals' friend . . .*

25

Or maybe this is better . . .

> *A girl of heart,*
> *A girl of grit,*
> *For the Agency, she's*
> *A perfect fit . . . ?*

Oh! Bother!"

He stopped, and Clover clapped in astonishment. "Thank you!"

The knight smiled sheepishly. "I know I'm rubbish. I used to be a bard, but I was never any good at it. I'm not terribly good at being a knight either."

"So you *are* a knight?"

"Oh, yes. Sir Walter Windsmith, at your service. And this is Phoebe, my pet phoenix." He pointed to the bird, who had stopped singing but was still clinging to the branch. "Phoebe's nearing her Ash Day. She's been very moody and tired because of it."

"Oh!" breathed Clover. A phoenix—a fire bird! That explained her glowing feathers and beautiful voice. Clover didn't know what an Ash Day was, but she remembered, from her research on eggs, that phoenixes didn't *have* eggs. When they died, they turned into ash, and a new phoenix rose from the ashes. Maybe that was an Ash Day? If so, no wonder poor Phoebe was scared.

"I don't have any experience with phoenixes, but . . ."

"Maybe Mr. Jams could help us, then . . . or the expert? Last I heard, Theodore was on a mission to bring a bird expert to the Agency."

Clover's back stiffened. "Actually, Oliver's an *egg* expert, so I don't think he'd be any use with a phoenix. I used to have a pet canary myself. Let me try." Picnic had clearly settled down, so she put him on the ground. "If you'll just hold Picnic's leash."

"Picnic?"

Clover gestured to the floating collar, which was now hovering near Sir Windsmith's feet.

"He's an invisible puppy," she explained.

"Ah! Remarkable!" Sir Windsmith rubbed his eyes. "Why, people always say seeing is believing, but certainly not in this case. He's the perfect subject for a poem. . . ."

"Sure," said Clover, handing him the leash. "But I think we should try to get Phoebe down first."

"Of course, of course!"

So Clover reached out her hand and called, "Here, Phoebe. Come here. I won't hurt you, I promise."

Phoebe ruffled her feathers. A few of them, mixed with ash, fell to the ground.

Clover tried again. "Here, Phoebe. Come on."

But the bird didn't budge. Even from the ground, Clover could see that the gold flecks in her eyes looked pale. She *was* scared.

"It'll be okay," said Clover softly. "At the Agency, we have a special rookery for phoenixes." It was true, though Clover had never been inside since they had never had a phoenix—not since she'd been there. "You'll really like it there. I *promise*."

Perhaps it was Clover's words or her steady outstretched hand, or maybe Phoebe could sense that Clover's heart was worried too. Whatever the reason, the phoenix lifted her wings, let go of the branch, and glided gracefully down to rest on Clover's shoulder.

Although Phoebe was large, she was surprisingly light. Clover

28

stayed perfectly still. She could feel the phoenix's talons through her cotton dress— not sharp but surprisingly warm, like being touched by a sunbeam. And for a moment, Clover felt like a sunbeam herself, happy and warm and shimmering.

"Oh! You did it! Wonderful work!" Sir Windsmith's face lit up as he stroked Phoebe's feathers. "We must get to the Agency. It is so important. Too much time has been lost as it is, what with Phoebe, and me blabbering on! You *will* show us the way, won't you?"

"Of course," Clover said, and took Picnic's leash. "Follow me."

As she led the way back to the Agency, she wasn't worried about the necklace or the summer ending or even Oliver.

After all, it's hard to worry when you have a phoenix on your shoulder and a knight by your side.

4

A Sword and a Suitcase

It wasn't long before the Agency came into view. "How quaint!" cried Sir Windsmith. "How charming!"

It really was. Clover loved Number 1 Dragon's Tail Lane: the tangle of vines and moss that covered the building, the thatched roof that was nibbled in places, and the fence that looked like a set of crooked teeth. And she loved Gump, the gnome who guarded the Agency at night. He looked just like a clay garden gnome, except, if you listened closely, you could hear him snoring. He was asleep now, in the sun, and Clover gave him a gentle pat as she opened the gate.

Sir Windsmith didn't follow her. He was lost in thought, a few steps back, murmuring, "Charming, darling . . . no, those don't rhyme. Quaint, faint . . ."

"Um . . . Sir Windsmith?" prompted Clover.

"Of course, of course!" he said, hurrying through. "Verse is my curse, you see, especially when there are urgent matters to attend to!"

Urgent? Clover looked at the phoenix on her shoulder and wondered just how soon Phoebe's Ash Day was. Would the bird burst into flames at any moment? Phoebe was so still and calm now, it was hard to imagine. But Mr. Jams would know.

When Clover opened the front door, she knew the hippocampus had arrived. The smell of salty seawater filled the room, and Oliver was soaking wet. She couldn't believe she'd missed it!

Mr. Jams had obviously just got off the phone. The receiver was still in one hand. A piece of toast was in the other. "Unfortunately, no one in the nearby sea kingdom has heard of anyone having lost a hippocampus," he said, "but the sea king there will spread the word."

"Good," said Oliver, rubbing his dripping hair with a towel. Then he stopped. "This towel has jam on it!"

"Oh, that must be from . . ." Mr. Jams said, raising his piece of toast. He caught sight of Clover, who

31

was unclipping Picnic from his leash. "Clover! Back so soon . . ." Then he saw the bird on her shoulder and Sir Windsmith standing behind her, and his eyes went wide.

"Troll's turnips! It can't be!" He leapt up, his piece of toast flying through the air and landing somewhere behind the desk.

"But it is! Sure as song," said Sir Windsmith. "My dear Theodore! Theodore Jams!"

He strode across the room and bent down, throwing his willowy arms around Mr. Jams in a hug.

When Sir Windsmith let go, Mr. Jams sputtered, "To . . . to what do I owe this unexpected pleasure?"

Clover pointed to Phoebe and was about to explain when Sir Windsmith spoke. To Clover's surprise, he said nothing about the phoenix. Instead he mumbled, "There's a problem, Theodore. A big one. I need your help. I need *Sir* Jams's help."

Sir Jams? But . . . but that would mean Mr. Jams was a knight. Mr. Jams wasn't a knight! Was he? Clover tilted her head to listen, and she noticed Oliver did too.

"You know I've given all that up," replied Mr. Jams with force.

"I know. And I wouldn't ask unless I had no choice. It's a long story."

"Perhaps we should talk upstairs, Walter," said Mr. Jams. "Clover, Oliver, please find some dried fire berries in the kitchen for the phoenix. I see Phoebe is nearing her Ash Day?" he said to his friend, leading him out of the front room.

"Yes, and she's much more on edge than last time. I think it has to do with the stress of these past days. . . ."

Their voices trailed away as they headed upstairs.

Oliver set down the towel and pushed up his glasses. "Hmm, interesting."

"What do you mean?"

"Well, as you know, Mr. Jams used to be a knight. A very well-known one. But my brother told me he renounced his knighthood because he refused to kill dragons."

Clover's mouth hung open.

"You didn't know that? He didn't tell you?" Oliver looked smug.

"Of course I knew," Clover quickly lied. "But why is Sir Windsmith here? I thought it was because of Phoebe."

The phoenix, still on Clover's shoulder, gave a little squawk.

"I'm not sure," said Oliver, adding, "Knightly endeavors, I presume." What exactly that meant, however, he wasn't sharing.

So Clover headed to the kitchen to find the fire berries for Phoebe. Oliver trailed after her.

The berries were bright red, like plump rubies, but Phoebe wouldn't eat any.

"She really IS nearing her Ash Day," said Oliver, giving the bird's feathers a stroke. "It's funny how books never explain . . ."

"Explain what?"

"Oh, nothing. I'm just observing her solemn demeanor. As well as all the other signs she exhibits: the dullish eyes; the ugly, crumbling feathers . . ."

Phoebe snapped her beak, and Oliver jerked his hand away.

"I don't think she likes being called ugly," said Clover.

"That's preposterous. She's just a bird. . . ."

Clover was about to argue when a loud thump came from upstairs. She peeked out of the kitchen and Oliver joined her. Raised voices echoed down from the tower, but she couldn't make out what they were saying.

"It sounds like they're fighting," she whispered.

"I can't imagine Mr. Jams fighting," Oliver replied in a hush.

"Neither can I."

Clover could feel Phoebe trembling and stroked her feathers gently.

A moment later, the voices grew louder as the door to Mr. Jams's room opened. Clover and Oliver ducked back into the kitchen.

Footsteps clumped down the stairs. "Very well!" puffed Mr. Jams. "If there's no other way. As you say, Walter, there's not a moment to lose. But bother! Bother and billyrocks! Clover! Oliver! Where are you?"

"Here," said Clover as she and Oliver stepped into the hall.

"Ah, good," said Mr. Jams. The shiny knight's helmet

Clover had seen earlier was tucked under his arm, and he was carrying his suitcase, a sock dangling from it.

Oh no, thought Clover. *Not again!*

"Oliver," said Mr. Jams, "please fetch me my sword. It is in the front room, on top of the bookshelf."

"Certainly," said Oliver, rushing off.

"Clover, take Phoebe to the rookery and put her in the middle of the sun since she's close to her Ash Day. She will stay here. It's best for her."

Middle of the sun? wondered Clover. Mr. Jams was clearly too distracted for questions, so she nodded, her mind whirling. She walked quickly but carefully, so as not to upset the phoenix, down the hall, past the small animals' room to a room right next to the stables—the rookery.

The rookery was surprisingly warm and filled with roosting pegs. The walls were painted a happy sky blue, and in one corner there was a beautiful mosaic of the sun, made up of small squares of mirror and tile. In the center of the sun was a round hole, also tiled. *So this was what Mr. Jams meant*, thought Clover. Gently she placed Phoebe in the mosaic's nest. "There you go," she said. There was just enough room for the bird. The phoenix ruffled her feathers and seemed to relax.

"See, I told you it's nice here," said Clover, stroking the bird's feathers again, her fingers tingling with warmth. They still tingled, even as she left the rookery.

When Clover returned to the front room, Mr. Jams was attaching his sword to his belt. The tip of the blade nearly touched the floor. "Humph, I'm too old for this," he muttered.

"This is the only option," said Sir Windsmith.

"I know," sighed Mr. Jams. Then he turned to Clover and Oliver and said, "As you must have gathered, Sir Windsmith and I are leaving on an important mission. I'm afraid we must depart immediately."

"But . . . but . . ." stammered Oliver. He seemed surprised, but Clover wasn't. Since she had started, Mr. Jams was always heading off on one mission or another—which was probably one of the reasons he had hired her.

"No time for questions," said Mr. Jams, and Clover knew that once again she wouldn't find out the details of the trip until he returned.

"You two must look after the Agency while I'm gone," he said, adjusting his sword.

You two? Now that was surprising. Clover had always been in charge of the Agency when Mr. Jams went away—by herself. It was something *she* was an expert at. Oliver had no experience running the Agency at all.

Mr. Jams, however, went on, "Work together and everything will be fine. There's plenty of bread and jam, and cinnamon and sugar, in the kitchen cupboard. And the supplies for the animals are well stocked. Most importantly, do you promise, both of you, to look after the Agency with all your hearts?"

"Of course!" Clover and Oliver burst out at the same time.

Clover flashed Oliver a wary look. He didn't seem to notice—which was probably a good thing. After all, Mr. Jams had asked her to get along with him, and so she should probably try. Maybe they could work together. Maybe Oliver would even help her polish those horns. This was a magical world, after all, and stranger things had happened.

After Sir Windsmith said good-bye to Phoebe (in verse, of course) and Mr. Jams packed one more jar of jam, the two set off.

Together, Clover and Oliver watched as the knights

marched down the path, the sound of Sir Windsmith's latest poem drifting back to them.

> *"Knights once again,*
> *Off to do a good deed.*
> *Luck be with us,*
> *And we shall succeed!"*

5

The Strange Symptoms

Clover and Oliver did manage to work together for the rest of the day. They were too shocked by Mr. Jams's sudden departure (and, for Clover, the discovery of his past as a knight) to argue.

When it came to introducing Clover to the hippocampus, though, Oliver was as much of a know-it-all as ever.

"I've adjusted the temperature of the room accordingly," Oliver announced.

The tank room was muggy and smelled like the seaside. The hippocampus was in the medium-sized tank in the center, the one Clover had prepared, by herself, the day before.

"Most hippocampi are the size of unicorns," said Oliver, "though this one"—he gestured with his wand—"is slightly larger. He's clearly a thoroughbred. You can tell from his scales. See how they are a continuous sea blue, from horse to fish? Observe the width of his fins. And look at his teeth, sharp as a shark's."

Actually, it was hard for Clover to get a good look at the hippocampus because the creature was swimming up and down, side to side, around and around, the whole time Oliver was speaking and gesturing. All she could see was a swirl of blue and green scales, fins, and mane. It made Clover dizzy!

"Are they usually this energetic?" she asked.

"Not to my extensive knowledge. Wild ones are unpredictable, of course, but domestic hippocampi are generally calm and well trained," said Oliver. "However, this one's given us nothing but trouble. Although clearly he *is* a pet, for you can see he is wearing a collar. Only his name, Neptune, is on it, with no address. I had a difficult time reading it. He won't stay still." At this, Oliver dramatically raised his hand with his wand in it, and . . .

WHOOSH!

42

Neptune leapt out of the giant tank and back down again.

SPLASH!

A wave of water spilled over, right onto Oliver.

"UGH!" sputtered Oliver, looking furious.

Clover was about to laugh when she noticed the hippocampus was now nosing the side of the tank, tossing his blue mane in the very same way Tansy the fairy horse did when she was showing off.

All at once, she understood. "Oliver, he's not badly trained. He's really *well* trained. Everything you've been doing with your wand, he's doing too. When you raised your wand, that was his cue to jump. I bet . . ."

Clover tried with her hands. She gestured to the left. Neptune swam to the left of the tank. She gestured up, and Neptune swam up. She gestured toward herself, and Neptune floated right against the tank, directly in front of them.

"Well . . ." sputtered Oliver. "That just proves my point that pet hippocampi are well trained. My conclusions are sound."

Clover would have rolled her eyes, but she was too mesmerized by the magical creature. At last she could get a good look at Neptune. He was the most beautiful and bizarre animal she had seen yet.

It wasn't his tail or teeth, or his mane tangled with seaweed and shells, or even the strange flippers he had instead of horse's legs that mesmerized her. It was Neptune's eyes—glassy green like the sea. It felt like she could see right through them and into his heart. *He misses his owner*, she thought. She hoped someone called in for him soon.

Now that they had learned that Neptune was trained, it was easy to feed him. Clover climbed the ladder at the side of the tank and gestured up. Neptune rose to the surface, and she fed him a bucket of sea-foam that Mr. Jams had left. Maybe she could convince Oliver to help her froth up some more later. Mr. Jams had told her what hard work it was to make—like mixing a really thick milk shake.

At the moment, though, Oliver was nowhere to be found. He had conveniently disappeared, claiming he needed to update Neptune's file. Clover assumed that, once again, he wouldn't return and was amazed when he came back to help her feed the rest of the animals their supper. Well, sort of help. He used a wand (his "Culinary" one, he said) to mix the food, but instead of making mush for the unicorns, it made cinnamon-raisin oatmeal. Plum took a particular liking to it, but Clover ended up having to make proper mush for the rest.

When she had cleaned up, she found Oliver sitting on the couch in the front room, his wand and bowls of different foods—mushy peas, mashed potatoes, soggy spaghetti, and even a bowl of soft strawberry ice cream—on the table in front of him. Dipity was in his lap. By Oliver's side, a potato biscuit was slowly disappearing. Picnic was cuddling there too. For a moment, it was as if Clover could see the puppy's little paws on either side of the treat. But, of course, she couldn't.

"What are you doing?" she asked Oliver.

"My Culinary wand is quite the disappointment," he said. "It really should be able to handle the animals' meal preparation, but . . ."

"You don't need a wand to make unicorn mush," she said.

"Yes, but I thought . . ." he started. "Never mind."

He shooed Dipity off his lap and began gathering up the bowls. He was about to pick up the last one, the ice cream, when he said, "Would you like some?"

Clover almost shook her head, but she was feeling strangely hot, whether from the mush-making or all the day's excitement she wasn't sure, and the ice cream *was* strawberry—her favorite. So she nodded, and he left it there, with a spoon that he drew from the pocket of his robes. She hoped it was clean. Before she could say thank you, he was gone.

Clover pulled Dipity and Picnic close, noticing all the crumbs the puppy had made on the couch. She would have to clean them up later. But right now, the ice cream was surprisingly good, and Dipity snuggly, and so things seemed, for a moment, strawberry sweet.

Clover's parents were working that night. They were often busy at the mayor's office, which was good because it meant that they didn't have time to pester Clover with questions about the Agency.

After fixing herself a tomato-and-cheese sandwich, Clover got ready for bed and noticed she was still wearing the necklace. She had forgotten to return it! She tried to take it off, but the clasp was still stuck.

In the light from her bedroom lamp, she saw that the sun charm looked shinier . . . prettier. Like a piece of dragon treasure. Clover wished she could show Emma. Emma would like it.

Too bad she would have to put it back. Tomorrow she'd have to find a way to undo the clasp and sneak it into Oliver's room.

❂

When Clover arrived at the Agency in the morning, all thoughts of the necklace quickly disappeared. The door was still locked. Oliver hadn't opened up yet! And he hadn't turned on the lights or fed the animals either! Clover knew because Picnic jumped on her the moment she stepped inside, his collar bobbing in the air. "Down," said Clover as he sniffed at her bag, looking for food. Dipity rubbed against her, meowing hungrily.

"Okay, okay. I'll get you guys some breakfast," she said, heading through the swinging door and into the hallway. "Humph, where is Oliver?"

At that very moment, he strode out of the phoenix rookery.

"There you are," he said to Clover.

"You know, you really should feed the animals right away," Clover replied. "Picnic's practically chewing on my leg. And open the door too."

"I was going to, but there's a bit of a situation . . ." he said.

Clover noticed Oliver was still wearing his pajamas (covered in a pattern of green-and-blue speckled eggs). His hair was sticking up all over the place, and his eyes were wide with worry.

"What do you mean, 'situation'?" asked Clover. "Is it Phoebe? Did she have her Ash Day?"

"Technically, yes," said Oliver. "But . . ."

"But what?"

"I think there's something you should see." He headed back inside the rookery.

Picnic and Dipity tried to go with him. "Sorry, guys," said Clover. "I promise I'll get you breakfast in a moment." She shooed them away, then warily followed Oliver.

The room smelled faintly of burning and was very quiet. So quiet she could hear her heart beating. What would she find in the tiled nest? She was almost too

afraid to look. She peeked nervously inside.

Ash. There was only a pile of ash.

"Where is she? What happened?" Clover demanded.

"By my estimation, based on the smoke, the bird flamed shortly after midnight."

"Bird? You mean, *Phoebe*."

"Yes, Phoebe. I checked on her as soon as I woke up. But . . ." he continued.

Clover gulped, "Oh no, is she . . . ?"

"No, no, she's not dead," Oliver said quickly. "Observe the ashes closely."

To Clover's relief, there was a faint glow coming from the center of them, pulsating like a heart.

"The ashes are most decidedly alive," said Oliver. "But the magic in them is faint, as though there is not enough to revivify the bird."

"Revivify?"

"'Revivify' means 'to bring back to life,'" replied Oliver, pushing up his glasses. "It is a very exact way of explaining the complex process—"

"Never mind," hurried Clover. "When will the ashes re . . . revivify?"

"I must admit," said Oliver, "I've never witnessed the process myself. I can't be entirely sure."

If only Mr. Jams were here, thought Clover. Why was he always gone when things went wrong? She took a deep breath and reminded herself that whatever mission he was on must be important since it required a helmet and sword. "Maybe Dr. Nurtch can help. She's a magical-animal vet and Mr. Jams's friend. I think we should phone her."

"No need," said Oliver. "I will find the cause, and the solution. I was about to head upstairs to consult my texts when you came in."

Clover bit her lip. She stared at the faint orangey-red glow in the center of the ashes. "Okay," she said. But it wasn't really okay. It wasn't okay at all.

While Oliver buried himself in his books, Clover fed the animals breakfast, starting, of course, with Dipity and Picnic. She gave them extra-big helpings and took a second bucket of sea-foam to Neptune, who was drifting in circles in his tank. She rubbed the hippocampus's wet muzzle for a while. It felt smooth and cool, the way she imagined a whale's nose might feel. In the stables, the unicorns looked out of sorts, and Clover swore their horns seemed duller and smaller than usual. *They really do need to be polished*, she thought. Maybe she could persuade Oliver to help. First, though, she needed her own breakfast. She was feeling a little out of sorts herself. She made some toast and sat down on the couch in the front room to cuddle with Dipity. Dipity always calmed her down. That was the kitten's magic.

But not today. Clover didn't feel calm. She felt worried. Something was wrong with Dipity. The tip of his tail seemed less green. In fact, it wasn't green at all. It was white!

Clover leaned closer and rubbed her eyes. Then she rubbed the kitten's tail. But the white didn't go away. Dipity mewed plaintively.

"Oliver!" Clover shouted. "You'd better come here—quick!"

He arrived in the front room, out of breath, in his robes now, and holding a massive tome in one hand and a wand in the other. "I found my Wellness wand. Thank goodness I packed it. But it will take me time to—"

"It's not that. It's this!" Clover pointed to Dipity's tail. The kitten flicked it this way and that, and she struggled to hold it still. "Look."

"Hmm . . ." puzzled Oliver, peering at the white fur. "Perhaps it's a case of transformatitis, or maybe chameleonitis."

"I think we should phone Dr. Nurtch," said Clover.

Oliver shook his head. "The kitten doesn't seem bothered by it, and I would much prefer to look it up myself, just as soon as I've solved our phoenix conundrum."

Clover was about to argue when . . . *BOOM! BOOM! BOOM!*

The loud knocks shook the Agency from top to bottom. She knew at once who it was.

"Better go get Picnic," she told Oliver. Before he had a chance to ask questions, Clover opened the door, tucking Dipity's tail into the crook of her elbow, out of sight.

It was Clover's friends the giants, rising a little higher than the Agency's roof.

Prudence was wearing an enormous frilly shirt that had I ♥ PUPPIES on the front in big pink letters. Her husband, Humphrey, was holding a bone the size of Clover's leg. It was nice to see that they were so eager about adopting Picnic. They had already filled out the paperwork, but because Picnic was still so young and such a rare animal, he couldn't be adopted yet. Luckily, the giants were willing to wait.

"Clover!" boomed Humphrey. "How delightful to see you. You're looking very"—he paused and squinted through his glasses—"bright today."

"Have you been getting too much sun?" Prudence broke in, peering at Clover's face too. "You should use some of my sunscreen. Humphrey, do you have that bottle?"

"Of course, my jewel box." Humphrey began to fiddle with his fanny pack, but Clover shook her head.

"I'm okay. I'm not sunburned. I'm just hot. Have you come to visit Picnic?"

"Yes; we were nearby, and we thought we'd bring him a treat."

"It was my idea," said Prudence petulantly.

"Of course it was, my bunny burrow," said Humphrey. "And such a good one too."

"Yes," agreed Clover, though she wasn't so sure. She didn't like to think where a bone that size had come from.

"Where is my puppy-wuppy?" cooed Prudence. "I do hope he's growing quickly. I will feel so much safer at night once he is guarding our beanstalk."

"It's only been a week," said Clover, "but he seems to be growing fine. He'll be ready to start bravery training when Lulu gets back." Lulu had helped Clover find Picnic, and she was really good with the puppy.

"Those leprechaun families are always off chasing rainbows," said Prudence. "So much traveling would tatter my nerves. . . ."

Just then, Oliver appeared in the doorway holding Picnic, the puppy's collar bobbing in his arms. "Um, Clover, I think there's something you should see . . ." he whispered. Before Oliver could explain, however, Prudence pointed to the collar and gave a happy shriek.

"Oh, there he is! Our darling!" She bent down and opened one hand, leaving Oliver no choice but to set Picnic down on her palm, which was as large as a coffee table.

Prudence raised Picnic up to her face. But her coo quickly turned into a gasp. "Oh my!"

"What's wrong, my treasure trove?" Humphrey asked. Examining Picnic, he exclaimed, "Oh dear!" He dropped the bone, and it landed with a loud thud that caused the ground to shake. "There, there. I'm sure it's merely a trick of the light." Humphrey rubbed his glasses on his shirt and peered at Picnic again.

"I do hope so," said Prudence. "Clover, *what* is the meaning of this?"

"Of what?" asked Clover, confused.

"Of this! Of these!" Prudence cried, setting Picnic back on the steps by Clover's feet. Clover looked down. There, beside her own feet, were paws. Golden-colored paws. Picnic's paws. They were visible!

"We want an *in*visible guard dog, not a visible one!" exclaimed Prudence. "What's the matter? Is he sick?"

Clover stammered, "He's . . . he's . . ."

"Yes, sick indeed," Oliver interrupted, stepping forward. "I'm a magical animal expert."

Prudence looked at him doubtfully. "Expert? Why, you look like a boy."

"I *am* a boy—Oliver Von Hoof the Third."

"Oh!" gasped Prudence. "Your family has been featured many times in *Magical Living* magazine."

"Then you must know that I come from a long line of magical animal experts." Oliver took out a wand, as if to prove his point.

"Is that a Wellness wand?" Prudence asked, seemingly impressed.

"Of course," said Oliver. "Picnic will be fine in no time."

Clover crossed her arms and shook her head in disbelief. Oliver was making things up! She opened her mouth to say so, but saw that Prudence and Humphrey had relaxed.

"See, my flower field," said Humphrey, putting his arm around his wife's shoulders, "there's nothing to worry about with both Clover and an *expert* taking care of our puppy." He turned to them. "We'll leave the bone here, then?"

"I don't know . . ." started Clover.

But Oliver broke in again, "Yes, of course."

Clover glared at him.

"Do let us know when Picnic gets better," said Prudence.

"I will," said Clover quickly, not wanting Oliver to have the last word. "I promise."

And so with a good-bye to Clover and Oliver and a wave to Picnic, the giants left, striding over the gate, leaving the bone in the middle of the front lawn, like a bad omen.

As they disappeared into the Woods, Oliver spoke. "I've come to the conclusion that we must call the veterinarian."

"Really?" Clover replied. "*You've* come to the conclusion? That's what *I*—"

She stopped herself, distracted by four golden paws bounding down the steps toward the gigantic bone.

"Picnic, not now! Come here!" she cried. But Picnic was already at the bone, and Clover swore she could see a little black nose sniffing it.

6

The Vet's Visit

Clover and Oliver waited anxiously in the front room for the vet. Oliver pulled out his Wellness wand. "This should help," he said, waving it vigorously over Dipity and then Picnic. But all the wand conjured was some chicken noodle soup. It didn't seem so helpful, especially since it was too hot for soup. Who ate soup in the summer anyway? Apparently, Oliver did. He was on his third bowl when they heard a strange sound outside.

There was a loud whooshing of wings, and bleating that sounded like a goat. Clover opened the door to an astonishing sight. It *was* a goat—sort of.

Just below the Agency's steps stood a very large, very white mountain goat with two pointed black horns and two wings that spread out above it like small fluffy clouds. It wore a saddle and a bridle, and Gump was standing beside it, holding its reins. The gnome didn't look too happy with the situation, especially since the goat was busy nib-bling the tip of his hat.

The goat's rider wasn't paying this any attention. In fact, it seemed she was used to the goat's behavior, for her clothes were nibbled and possibly her hair too. It was hard to tell about the hair, though, because it looked like a scraggly patch of moss on a rock. Actually, every-thing about the woman reminded Clover of a rock. Her skin was grayish, her nose large and lumpy, and her shoulders square. Was she a troll?

Mr. Jams had never said. Clover had met all types of magical folk at the Agency, from ghosts to leprechauns. Troll or not, this was definitely the veterinarian. Around her neck was a large stethoscope, and her bag had a patch on it that read MAGICAL-ANIMAL SUPPLIES: MEDICINES, MIXTURES, AND MOXTURES. What moxtures were, Clover didn't know.

Dr. Nurtch's eyebrows were the same color as her hair, and they rose up in one piece when she saw Clover.

"At last. It's good to finally meet you," said the vet, shaking Clover's hand with force. Clover had missed Dr. Nurtch's last visit, to check on the magical kittens, because the vet had arrived before the sun was up. "But schedules are schedules and mine is beyond ridiculous. Good thing Nanny here is an early riser," she said, gesturing to the winged goat. "Today we had an appointment at dawn. Another case of a wand-happy witch, trying to see if she could get her bat to speak Latin. Of course *that* was a smart idea," Dr. Nurtch huffed with a roll of her eyes. "I've never seen a bat so confused. Poor thing was reciting the alphabet upside down and backward."

"'Sense not spells,' right?" said Clover.

Dr. Nurtch smiled, revealing a large gap in her teeth. "Right you are," she said. "Now what's the problem here?"

Clover invited the vet in and showed her Dipity and Picnic, who were both on the couch. She started to explain when Oliver interrupted, "I thought at first it might be a case of transformatitis, but, as Dr. Gibbs

62

says, transformatitis occurs within an hour and it has already been three. Dr. Gibbs is a family friend of the Von Hoofs, you know. He even gave me . . ." Oliver reached into his pocket and started to pull out a wand.

Dr. Nurtch held up one hand to stop him from continuing, then set her bag on the table. When she opened it, Clover saw a pair of giant tweezers, a teeny-tiny bandage roll, and a syringe that zigzagged like a lightning bolt. She wondered what else was inside. "I've heard of Gibbs," said the vet. "Uses a Wellness wand, I hear. They seldom work. Can't stand those things."

Oliver looked deflated, much to Clover's delight. He stuck his wand back in his pocket. Dr. Nurtch didn't seem to notice and began to check Dipity. First she examined his fur, peering closely at his tail, and then at a white patch on his stomach.

"I don't think that was there before," said Clover.

"Hmm," replied Dr. Nurtch, pulling out a thermom-eter from her bag and placing it in Dipity's ear. After a moment, she checked it. "Temperature seems good." She held her stethoscope against Dipity's side and lis-tened. "Heart rate regular, breathing too. How's his appetite?"

"Normal," replied Clover.

"Kit's got magic?"

"He can calm people, and animals too."

"It's a rare talent that is correctly referred to as—" started Oliver.

"Yes, yes, proximal tranquility," said Dr. Nurtch, waving Oliver quiet again, much to his dismay, as she took what looked like a long black wand from her bag.

"A wand! You *do* have one!" Oliver cried triumphantly.

Dr. Nurtch shot him a withering glare. "This is NOT a wand. This is a magimeter, of course."

What exactly a magimeter was, Clover didn't know, and clearly neither did Oliver, so she watched curiously as Dr. Nurtch held it over Dipity. After a moment, the magimeter began to glow a faint yellow. "Hmm. Low." She clucked her tongue and moved on to Picnic before Clover could ask what that meant.

Picnic, of course, was much harder to examine, but since his nose and paws were visible, and the golden tips of his floppy ears were now too, it made things easier for the vet. She checked his nose first, then pressed her stethoscope on what had to be his side. "Heart rate seems good," she noted. She took out a square magnifying glass and peered through it. "No fleas either."

"Do magic animals get fleas?" asked Clover.

"Of course," said Oliver knowingly. "Dragon fleas

spit itchy fire. Unicorn fleas are sparkly so they blend in with unicorn hair. Invisible fleas shall be part of chapter seven in my volume on invisible animals."

"Well, our animals don't have fleas," said Clover confidently. "I keep them clean."

Dr. Nurtch wasn't listening. She held the magimeter over Picnic. It glowed a faint yellow. The vet clucked her tongue again.

"What does it mean?" asked Clover.

"Not sure yet," said Dr. Nurtch. "Except this is a magical malady of some sort. Have any other animals been affected?"

Oliver shook his head, but Clover said, "What about Phoebe?"

"The phoenix is a separate case," said Oliver.

"What's this?" asked Dr. Nurtch. "I didn't know you had a phoenix here."

"We're just looking after her for a bit," said Clover. "Well, we were, but now . . ."

While Clover explained, Dr. Nurtch's eyebrows scrunched closer and closer together. When Clover was done, the vet insisted on seeing Phoebe's ashes, which got an orange color reading from the magimeter and a double tongue cluck from the vet, who then declared she must check the rest of the animals as well.

"I can show you around," said Oliver.

Dr. Nurtch shouldered her bag. "Best have the one most familiar with the animals. Come, Clover. Let's start with the unicorns."

Clover couldn't help but smile.

As it turned out, there wasn't much she had to do for the vet, except hold her heavy bag. After the stables, they moved to the tank room, where the vet checked Neptune's teeth, nose, and tail too, the hippocampus obediently lifting it out of the water for her. "Very well trained," commented Dr. Nurtch. After collecting a sample of the hippocampus's scales, she held the magimeter over him. Instead of a pale yellow, it glowed a faint pink. "Hmm, better," said Dr. Nurtch.

Then they were on to the small animals' room. The only animals the vet needed some help with were the fairy horses. Dr. Nurtch's fingers were too big for the tiny thermometer and stethoscope that were required to check the fairy horses' temperatures and heart rates, so Clover got to use them, holding each horse on one hand and the tiny tools in her other. "Good job," said Dr. Nurtch. "You've a pixie's touch." Clover felt proud.

With every animal, Dr. Nurtch used the magimeter. Each time it glowed a faint pink, except for the

salamanders, which glowed turquoise. Did pink mean normal? But then what did turquoise mean?

When they returned to Oliver, after scrubbing thoroughly in the washing room, Clover found out.

"Generally low magic levels all around. Except the fire salamanders," announced Dr. Nurtch, with a sniff through her lumpy nose. "They're fine. The other animals' readings are better than Picnic's and Dipity's, but still not normal. You said Mr. Jams is gone? That's a shame. Not that you aren't capable, Clover. I know you are. It's just that I've never seen anything quite like this. The hippocampus recently arrived, correct?"

"I *told* Mr. Jams we weren't taking proper precautions with Neptune, though he insisted it was fine," said Oliver. "Newcomers do tend to be the bearers of blights."

Clover couldn't help but think, *You're new too*, though she didn't say it aloud.

"Hmm, well if Mr. Jams thought Neptune was fine, I'm apt to believe him. Still, I'll do some research on waterborne illnesses. Perhaps consult A. Brook—"

"Is it the *Encyclopedia of Magical Marine Mammals*?" asked Oliver excitedly.

"*Brook*," said Dr. Nurtch, looking, to Clover's delight, more than a little annoyed now. "As in Aloysius

Brook, a vet of the sea, who's a good friend of mine. Yes, I think I'll speak with him. In the meantime"—Dr. Nurtch opened her bag and rifled through it—"these are Pocus Pills," she said, producing a round bottle as big as Clover's fist. "Try 'em first. They usually stop loss of magic. Give one to each animal—even the salamanders, just in case."

Then she took out another bottle that was narrow and long. "If that doesn't work, this is Extra-Strength Presto Powder. It's vile stuff; animals don't usually like it. But it will boost the magic of an animal in an urgent situation. 'Course you should phone me if things get worse. Or if things get better. I'd like to have an update either way. Here's my card, as a reminder."

She handed it to Clover. It read:

DR. NETTIE NURTCH, MAGICAL-ANIMAL VETERINARIAN
THE HILLSIDE HOSPITAL
JUST BEFORE BEYOND, THE WOODS
999-111-SENSE

"What about Phoebe?" asked Clover. How were they supposed to give ashes medicine?

"Blow on the embers. Gently, mind. That should

69

help. And I noticed one of the kits has been adopted. Was that recently?"

"Just yesterday," said Clover.

"I handled the adoption," said Oliver. "I'll phone Sabine to make sure the young grimalkin is healthy."

Sabine must be the witch's name, thought Clover.

They were interrupted by a loud bleating outside.

"Time to go," said Dr. Nurtch, closing her bag with a snap. "Nanny is good at keeping me on schedule. I've got to check up on Snort. Remember him, Clover?"

Of course she remembered Snort! He was the baby dragon she'd adopted out earlier in the summer. "Is he okay?" she asked.

"Oh, yes. He's got that troublesome fire under control now, with the help of Henry. It's just a normal checkup. Not like this." Dr. Nurtch clucked her tongue again. "It's really too bad Mr. Jams isn't around. That Jams is always off fixing one sticky situation or another. Jams . . . Sticky . . ." She chuckled at her own joke, and Clover was surprised how very similar to Nanny her laugh sounded.

While Dr. Nurtch cleaned her supplies in preparation for her next appointment, Clover fetched Nanny from Gump, who looked relieved to see the goat go. Nanny nibbled at one of Clover's braids. When she moved on to the collar of Clover's dress, Clover was

70

sure she saw Gump smirk. But before she could say anything to him, she felt a tug on the necklace. Nanny was nibbling at the chain!

"Stop that! You'll get me into trouble," said Clover, quickly pulling it away from the goat. She still hadn't returned the necklace. There hadn't been time! *I'll just keep wearing it for now*, she thought. *Until things settle down*. After all, Oliver hadn't noticed it was missing. For such a know-it-all, he wasn't very observant.

Clover had just tucked the charm out of sight when Dr. Nurtch emerged with Oliver tagging along behind her. Slinging her bag across her square shoulder, the vet settled into the saddle and was off, but not without some final advice.

As Nanny lifted into the air, wobbling a little under the weight of the vet, Dr. Nurtch hollered, "Remember, two can be better than one—unless, of course, you're a three-headed dog."

It was the first thing the vet had said that didn't really make sense.

7

Pills and Powders

The Pocus Pills were tiny and very colorful, like the sprinkles on cupcakes. They even smelled sugary. As far as pills went, they didn't seem so bad. But the animals didn't want to take them. Picnic wouldn't stay still long enough, and Dipity turned up his nose. Clover thought holding the salamanders would help her give them their pills, although she worried they might be too hot to hold, hotter than baked potatoes. They weren't. But they didn't take their pills either. They seemed to like being picked up so much, they fell asleep as soon as they were in her hands.

Clover needed another plan. When she was putting the salamanders back in their tank, she remembered how she used to feed Esmeralda the toad her vitamins, by mixing them in with some squashed flies. Maybe disguising the pills would work?

So Clover slid a Pocus Pill into a hollowed-out pepper—and Flame actually ate it! Ash ate his too. She used the same trick with the rest of the animals, hiding the pills in their favorite foods, except for Neptune.

Since he was so well trained, Clover didn't have to hide the pill, which was a good thing because she wasn't sure what to hide it in. Sea-foam wouldn't work.

For the unicorns, she hid the pills in apple slices. They gobbled them up. All except Plum. He kept nudging his bucket, which still smelled like the cinnamon-raisin oatmeal from the night before.

"Now *you're* being picky?" Clover sighed.

Plum whinnied, but Clover looked at him sternly and held out the apple slice. "Eat up. You need this." And at last Plum did.

After Oliver had phoned Sabine and found out Blizzard was fine, he volunteered to blow on the ashes in the rookery while Clover gave the animals their medicine. When she checked, the ashes didn't seem to be glowing any brighter. To distract herself from worrying, Clover began work on the new Wish Book, while Oliver went upstairs to research magical-water-animal diseases.

The Wish Book was an important part of the Agency. It was for customers to record requests for animals the Agency didn't have. The old Wish Book had been chewed to pieces by Picnic, so Mr. Jams ordered a new one. With a big gilt cover, it looked identical to the first, except that its pages were blank. Clover's job was to copy as much as she could still read from the old book.

It was a time-consuming task, even if she was getting better at using the drippy quill pen. The one good thing was that she didn't have to record any requests that had been filled. She came across quite a few, and each one made her happy. Especially this entry: *Miss*

Opal, fortune-teller / Looking for a mood creature, firefly preferred. There was a check mark beside it that Clover had put there herself at the beginning of the summer.

I wonder if Miss Opal could see into the future and tell me how long Oliver is going to be at the Agency? And what about me? Will I be able to stay on once school starts? She was tempted to give the fortune-teller a call, but if she was going to ask for a fortune, shouldn't she ask about the animals? Maybe the fortune-teller could "see" what their sickness was. Wasn't THAT really what mattered? Then she remembered that fortune-tellers—especially Miss Opal—often spoke in riddles, and what she needed right now was a clear answer.

Clover didn't notice her quill pen was dripping until Oliver walked in.

"You're getting ink everywhere," he commented. "And your penmanship . . ."

"Don't you have other things to do?" asked Clover, her cheeks flaring. "Why are you here?"

"It's the animals' suppertime," he replied. "I've set my Alarm wand to alert me to all the mealtimes at the Agency. It is very handy."

Clover rolled her eyes, but it *was* time to feed the animals their suppers, so she put the book away.

The animals didn't seem better. Just the opposite, in fact. Both of Picnic's ears were visible and the tips of his wings too. The fairy horses looked bigger and the hippocampus smaller. Definitely smaller. His collar had slipped off and was lying in the seaweed at the bottom of the tank.

"Wait until the morning," said Oliver. "It's common knowledge that Pocus Pills need at least twelve hours to take full effect."

Clover hoped that for once Oliver, Mr. Know-It-All, was correct.

✺

That night during supper, Clover thought of Emma. Although Emma read lots, like Oliver, she never acted like a know-it-all. She was nice to everyone. Clover realized she hadn't received a postcard from Emma in a while. *She's probably too busy making lots of new friends at Pony Camp*, thought Clover.

Would Emma seem different when she saw her again in the fall? Clover knew she herself had changed. Would they still be best friends? And how would she keep the

Agency a secret—especially if she was still volunteering there?

As though her mom could read her mind, she said, "Have you thought about continuing at the Agency when school starts, Clover? I know you've been enjoying it."

"I'd *love* to," replied Clover. "And I really want to. But there's another volunteer and—"

"The more help the merrier, I always say," said her dad. "Your mother and I couldn't imagine working without each other."

Clover didn't say anything, but she had no trouble at all imagining working without Oliver.

❈

"Oliver, what's going on?" Clover cried the next morning, when she entered the Agency to the sound of loud barking.

Was it Picnic? He never barked! The noise was coming from the small animals' room. There, she found Oliver standing on a chair beside one of the large empty cages at the back of the room. Picnic perched on the top edge of the cage. It *was* him barking. And no wonder. He was stuck.

He was almost completely visible (and the cutest puppy she had ever seen), with sunshiny fur and floppy ears, and two feathery golden wings that he was flapping frantically with every bark. But the wings weren't lifting him off the top of the tank. They seemed much smaller than the wings Clover had felt when he was invisible. Just as Picnic was appearing, his wings were *disappearing*!

"He must've flown up there but now he can't fly down," Clover thought aloud.

"I know! I've been trying every appropriate spell!" said Oliver breathlessly, turning to Clover, a wand in his hand. He paused when he saw her. "Oh, you look—"

Now wasn't the time for another one of his lectures! "Well, no wonder he won't come down," Clover interrupted, "not when you're pointing *that* at him. Here, let me."

Clover stepped on a chair too. "Jump down. Come on, Picnic. There's a good puppy," she coaxed.

Picnic stopped flapping.

"Come on. . . ." Clover reached up, and the puppy leaned forward and leapt into her arms. He gave her a happy lick and then squirmed free and bounded off. He

really was the cutest puppy she had ever seen. But he wasn't supposed to BE seen!

The magic kittens weren't displaying any of their magic, and Dipity, lying on top of their cage, was all white except for one green ear and green paws. Clover couldn't see the fire salamanders at first, until she looked closer and realized they were hiding in the shade, which was very unusual for such heat-loving creatures. *Maybe they're sick now too*, she thought.

The fairy horses were the worst off, all squished in their cage like sardines. Where before the ferns were like trees to them, now the horses towered over them like giants. Tansy's nose even reached the top of the cage, and she was licking at the latch. Butternut and

Buttercup were pushing against each other, vying for space. And Acorn was standing in the water dish because there was no other room left.

"We have to get them out of there," said Clover.

"But where will they go?" asked Oliver.

"In the stables, I guess." Clover opened the cage and lifted Tansy out. She was heavier than Dipity. "Don't just stand there. Help me."

Oliver put his wand away and awkwardly lifted Buttercup out. Right away, she bared her teeth and nipped his hand.

"Ah!" he yelled, stumbling back and knocking into Clover.

"Watch out!" she scolded. Luckily, she was holding Tansy tight and didn't drop the fairy horse.

Oliver, on the other hand, was clearly not holding Buttercup properly. The dappled horse jumped out of Oliver's arms and landed gracefully on the floor. Seeming only too happy to be free, she began to prance around the room, whinnying loudly.

"What should I do?" cried Oliver.

"Catch her!" said Clover.

So Oliver chased Buttercup, who began to gallop, tossing her mane like a flag. Dipity watched, looking amused.

It WAS pretty funny, but Tansy was getting heavy. "Come on!" said Clover.

Oliver huffed to a stop. "Really, these animals are not well trained!"

"It's not the animals. It's you," she said.

Oliver's face fell, and Clover almost felt bad. Then Buttercup pranced by, and Oliver got his arms around her at last. "Aha!" he said smugly, lifting her back up.

"Good," said Clover. "Come on."

The not-so-fairy horses were actually A LOT heavier than Dipity. By the time Clover got Tansy into a stall in the stables, her arms ached. Oliver put Buttercup in the same stall. The two horses happily explored, sniffing the hay and buckets and swishing their tails.

The unicorns were not as pleased. They looked bewildered, and it was no wonder. Their horns were half the size they used to be. And it wasn't just their horns that were changing. They were changing colors too. Instead of milky white, they were an assortment of hues and patterns, cream and spotted, chestnut and patched, just like the horses at Emma's Pony Camp. "Oliver, those pills didn't help at all," said Clover.

"It is VERY perplexing," he agreed.

"It's more than that," said Clover. "It's time for the

vet. You move Acorn and Butternut. I'm going to call Dr. Nurtch."

The phone rang a few times and Clover fiddled with the charm, worried that the vet might be out. Dipity hopped up on the desk.

"Do you know what's going on?" Clover asked her kitten. Dipity didn't respond as he usually would, with a twitch of his tail. He just mewed like an ordinary cat and curled up on the desk. Clover rubbed behind his ears as the phone went to the answering machine: "You've reached Dr. Nettie Nurtch," said a gruff voice. "I'm either out on a call, or—"

Clover was about to give up when there was a click and a loud bleating in the background, then, "Shush, Nanny. . . . Hello? What ails your animal?"

"Dr. Nurtch, it's Clover at the M.A.A.A. The pills didn't work. Picnic is more visible, and the fairy horses are huge."

"They're losing their magic, no doubt about it."

Clover stammered, a terrible thought swirling in her head, "Are . . . are they becoming . . . ordinary?"

"I don't have experience with ordinary animals, but it appears so," said Dr. Nurtch, sounding less gruff and more worried as she went on, almost as if she was talking to herself. "Can't say I'm surprised, what with what's happened here."

"What do you mean?"

"My Nanny's not herself either. It seems she too has the sickness. It must be very contagious. Have you tried the powder?"

"No, not yet."

"Give it a go. Dust the animals with it. That should help. Watch out for sneezing. I'll visit by foot tomorrow, first thing. Rest assured, I'll find a cure."

"Okay," said Clover, taking heart.

"But you best put up a quarantine sign."

"Quarantine? What's that?" asked Clover.

"You know, shut down the Agency. Don't let any animals in or out. And be extra careful with cleanup. Can't let this spread, especially when we don't know what we're dealing with."

Immediately Clover's hope faltered. "Really? But . . ."

84

Too late. There was a loud bleating again, followed by another click, and Dr. Nurtch was gone.

"How will I make the sign? I don't even know how to spell 'quarantine,'" finished Clover, slumping in her chair.

She could ask Oliver. He would know. But she didn't want to.

No matter how it was spelled, "quarantined" still meant that the Agency, *her* Agency, was closed.

8

Quarantined!

That night, after a long afternoon of powdering the animals and being sneezed on, even by the fire salamanders (who she didn't know *could* sneeze), Clover lay in bed and gazed at her memory wall, where she'd pinned up pictures of her past pets. She'd had lots of animals before coming to the Agency—ordinary ones, of course, including a fish, a puppy, and a bird. But they had all gotten lost or chosen other places to live. She'd never had a single one fall ill. And now she had a whole Agency full of sick animals, including Dipity. What would happen if Dipity got sicker and sicker? If all his magic disappeared?

What about Phoebe? Was it too late for her to rise from her ashes? If she didn't, would she die?

Clover's head was so full of questions, and she felt so uncomfortably hot—and prickly too, like she had dusted herself with the Presto Powder. Even opening the window to let in a breeze didn't help. She tossed and turned all night, dreaming of the Agency.

✦

As soon as the sun rose, she got up and headed to the Woods and down the path, hoping another visit from the vet would put her mind at ease.

But the vet wasn't waiting at the Agency when she arrived. There were two customers there instead.

At least, she thought it was just two, but as she neared the door, she realized there were two regular-size people and two teeny-tiny others—with wings. Fairies! One of the fairies was flitting around in front of the QUARANTINED sign.

"No animals accepted!" cried the fairy in a deeper voice than Clover expected. "This is ridiculous!"

The fairy was about as tall as a thumb, and, though there was a shimmer about him because his wings were beating so fast, he was clearly NOT the twinkly kind who grants wishes or collects teeth. *This* fairy was dressed in a button-up shirt with a teensy tie.

"Well, Papa, we'll just have to keep them, then," piped the second fairy, who was even smaller and standing on the top step, holding a box the size of a postage stamp. He was dressed very un-fairylike as well, in a striped shirt and shorts, with his blond hair sticking out of a tiny baseball cap.

The regular-size customers—who, judging by the way they were dressed, were obviously witches—seemed equally distraught by the sign. "I really wanted you to meet him, Stelly. He's SOO cute!"

The other witch, presumably Stelly, sighed. "It's okay, Sabby. But I *was* really hoping to see those animals. I am just dying to get a cute pet like your Blizzy."

Sabby? Blizzy? It must be that witch who adopted Blizzard. What was her name again? "Sabine?" Clover said at last.

The customers turned around. It *was* Sabine, the witch Oliver had helped with an adoption. She was wearing a black outfit, patterned this time with cobwebs, and holding a bottle of lemonade. Her friend Stelly looked like she might be Sabine's twin. She was dressed in the same outfit, but instead of long black hair with a streak of purple, her hair was purple with a streak of black.

Sabine looked Clover up and down. "Do you work here too, helping Oliver?"

"Actually Oliver helps *me*. I've been here all summer," said Clover.

"Oh!" said Sabine. "You're *sooo* lucky. He's *sooo* smart. And I bet he thinks those sparkles you're wearing are spiderific!"

"What do you mean? I'm not wearing any sparkles," said Clover, puzzled.

"I mean, I totally understand if you have a crush on him too," continued Sabine.

"I don't!" said Clover.

Sabine just rattled on, "So, what's going on? What's with the sign? Are the animals sick? What about Ollie? Is he sick?"

Clover shook her head.

"That's good. 'Cause I brought him some of my lemonade."

"I'm sorry, but the Agency is closed. No one can go inside."

"But we MUST leave our mice here," burst the fairy father.

Clover had already forgotten about the fairies! "I'm sorry, Mr. . . . ?" she started.

"Mr. Flitmore. Maury Flitmore," said the fairy.

"I'm Frances," said the fairy boy. "My mimimouse just had these babies."

Clover, and Sabine and Stelly as well, knelt down and peered closely into the box the boy held up.

"AW!" cried Stelly. Even Clover was tempted to gush. Inside were three of the tiniest mice she had ever seen—the size of peas, so small you couldn't even see their whiskers. Fairy mice! She had never considered that fairies would have pets other than fairy horses—but of course!

She remembered there was tiny soap for mimimice in the washing room. The Agency must have had some up for adoption at one point.

"Papa says I can't keep them."

"We certainly can't. We're moving tomorrow, to a smaller house." Maury flitted close to Clover's face, his arms crossed. "There must be something you can do."

"I'm sorry," said Clover, and to be polite she added, "And you too, Sabine and Stelly. Perhaps you could come back in a few days?"

"In a few days we'll be forests away!" cried Maury. "We'll just have to release them into the Woods."

"Please, Papa, no!" cried Frances. "What if a big bug finds them . . . ?"

"What if I took them?" interrupted Stelly. "They are *super* cute. I mean, I *was* thinking about getting a pet today."

"That's a *toad*ally great idea!" exclaimed Sabine. "I mean, we'd have to keep them away from Blizzy, of course, but—"

"Really? You really want them?" said Frances.

"Oh, yes!" said Stelly.

"Is it okay, Clover?" asked Sabine.

Clover wasn't sure what to say—or even if she should

say anything. She hadn't brought in the mimimice, so it wasn't really an adoption, was it? "Um . . ."

Maury made the decision for her. "Of course it's okay. We would be grateful if you took the mice, young witch." He turned and glared at Clover. "Humph, this is not the Agency I expected. I heard that the non-magical girl who works here is good. I must say, I am VERY disappointed." And with that, he took the box from his son and handed it to Stelly, then ushered her down the path, explaining, along with Frances, proper mimimice care. Clover felt awful.

"Don't feel down," said Sabine, lingering behind. "Fairies are always having freak-outs."

"Really?" said Clover. "I didn't think *fairies*—"

"Well, like my mom always says, glitter can hide what's really inside." Clover was about to nod when Sabine went on, "But not with Ollie. He's not glittery at all. He's, like, an actual expert. He's *sooo* amazing! Anyway, can you give this to him? And tell him I was here?" She handed her bottle of lemonade to Clover and, with a flip of her hair, headed down the path.

Clover shouldered her bag and was about to head inside when she noticed two new people—burly-looking men, each pushing a wheelbarrow—coming up the path.

More customers? she thought with a groan. She really needed to get to the animals. But then she saw what was in one of the wheelbarrows and she couldn't help but be excited. Although one wheelbarrow was empty, the other was filled with water. And in the water sat . . .

A mermaid!

Her tail, hanging over the end of the wheelbarrow, was greeny-blue, and so was her hair. Shell jewelry decorated her neck and wrists, and her ears too.

"Hello? Are you Jams? Is Neptune here? A sea dweller told me he was," said the mermaid breathlessly, pressing a wet towel to her forehead when she reached the bottom of the steps. Her lips were chapped and her cheeks flushed. "I've come such a long way."

"I'm not Mr. Jams, but I work here. I'm Clover. And, yes, we do have Neptune. He came in two days ago. But—"

The mermaid gave her no chance to continue. "Oh, thank the Seven Seas!" she gushed. "I've been so worried about him. My name's Meg."

"Princess Meg," added the porter pompously.

"You're a princess?" asked Clover.

"Yes," said Meg. "But we sea princesses are nothing like land princesses. Why, I've heard dreadful things

93

about how they treat their pets. All they really care about is outshining their friends. You're not a princess, are you?"

"Me? Of course not . . ."

"Oh," said Meg, "I thought maybe because you're so bright. . . . It looks like you're using Glamor Glitter."

Clover shook her head. Why was everyone commenting on her looks? "I'm NOT a princess," she said firmly. "I'm just an ordinary girl, a volunteer here—"

"It must just be the light, then," interrupted the mermaid. "I'm not used to it, you know. Well, I'm glad you're not a princess. I would never trust a land princess with a pet. There's nothing I wouldn't do for Neptune. That's how I lost him, you know. I had found a field of sea grass, his favorite place to play. He was so excited, I let him off his lead rope. Then a whale passed by and startled him, and Neptune swam away. When I heard he was here, I came at once, though arranging transportation is always difficult."

"I'm afraid—" started Clover.

"The porter can carry me in if he must. I can't wait to see Neptune."

"You . . . you can't," said Clover.

The mermaid's tail twitched. "Why not?"

"The Agency is quarantined." Clover pointed to the sign. "The animals are all sick, including your pet."

Now the mermaid's tail began to tremble. "Neptune's sick? I really *must* see him!"

"I'm so sorry, I . . . I can't let you," said Clover. Meg clearly loved her pet, and Clover didn't want her to see Neptune so transformed by illness. Meg might not even think it was Neptune at all.

Tears began to spill out of her eyes, but not tears like Clover's, tears of pearls! "Neptune is my pet. It's not fair. *You* get to see him!" The pearls fell to the ground, bouncing down the path.

"But that's different. I . . . I work here . . ."

"And *I'm* his owner. I want to see him. Please?" sobbed Meg.

"I really can't. . . ."

"You're speaking to a sea princess," said the porter. "What she commands must be obeyed."

Clover gulped.

"Please?" she sobbed. "Please, please?"

"Tomorrow!" burst Clover. "Come back tomorrow. Tomorrow Neptune will be better. I promise!"

The promise flew out of her mouth like an escaping bird. And there was no getting it back. Her face burned,

96

and she wished she had a cool towel like the mermaid. Or a sea to sink into. But she didn't. All she had was the prickly-hot feeling of making a promise she didn't know how to keep, even if it did make the mermaid feel better.

Meg sniffled. Her tears stopped. "Tomorrow," said the mermaid with a nod. "I'll come back tomorrow."

And, so, with a final sniffle and a wave, she and her porters were gone, out of the sun and back into the shady Woods, leaving pools of pearls behind them.

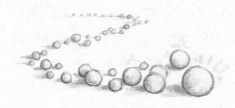

9

Only Ashes

At last, Clover opened the Agency door. Oliver was waiting for her. "Here," she said, pressing the lemonade into his hands. "This is from Sabine."

He took the bottle, but instead of thanking her he said, "The Presto Powder hasn't worked. The animals are extremely . . . extremely"—he pushed his glasses up his nose—"*ordinary.*"

Oliver was right. In the small animals' room, the kittens still mewed and tumbled with each other, but without soaring, somersaults, or sparks. The salamanders lay in their water dish, trying to cool off. In the stables, the unicorns were a medley of colors, their horns completely gone. But Clover couldn't thoroughly check any of the animals because she had to deal with the fairy horses. The fairy horses were definitely NOT fairy-size. They no longer fit comfortably in one stall, and Clover struggled to move them into individual ones. Oliver was trying to help but kept getting in the way, so Clover sent him to go make ice cubes for the salamanders with his Wellness wand. The temperature in the salamanders' tank wasn't adjustable, and for the first time ever, they were overheating. Meanwhile, she finished with the fairy horses and then checked on Neptune.

The big tank was empty. *Oh no*, thought Clover. *He's disappeared!*

Then . . . something caught Clover's eye. A slight movement at the bottom of the tank. She knelt down and saw a palm-size sea horse, like the kind she'd seen in the aquarium at home, peeking out from a cluster of seaweed. She peered in through the glass. The sea horse had the same green eyes as Neptune; that was all. She gestured up, but Neptune floated away. He didn't remember his commands.

Now she would *never* be able to keep her promise to Meg. She had to talk to Dr. Nurtch.

Clover hurried to the front room.

Oliver was there, waving a wand with one hand and holding open a book with the other. His hair was sticking up, and he was muttering different spells.

"I thought you were making ice cubes," said Clover.

"I can't," replied Oliver. "My wands aren't working. Not the Wellness wand, or the Culinary one. Not even my Clothes Folding wand."

"This is not the time for clothes folding!" exclaimed Clover. "Forget about your wands. We have bigger problems. Neptune's a sea horse. The unicorns are ponies, and have you checked on Phoebe's ashes?"

Oliver shook his head.

"Well, you'd better. I'm going to phone Dr. Nurtch. What's taking her so long?"

The phone rang and rang and rang.

It didn't switch over to the answering machine.

Clover hung up and tried again.

The phone rang and rang and rang once more, and then there was a click. Someone had picked up. "Hello?" asked Clover.

Instead of a reply, there was a racking cough on the other end.

"Dr. Nurtch, is that you?"

There was no reply, only more coughing. And then the line went dead.

Was that Dr. Nurtch? She sounded terrible! Was something wrong with her? Was she sick too? There was only one thing to do. If the vet couldn't come to her, Clover had to go to the vet. She picked up Dr. Nurtch's card, which was on the desk, and checked the address:

THE HILLSIDE HOSPITAL

Just Before Beyond, The Woods

She'd seen a sign for Beyond at the crossroads. If it was just before Beyond, then it couldn't be too far away.

She hurried to the rookery to tell Oliver.

Oliver was standing in front of the nest of ash, his wands littered around him on the floor like sticks. Except for one. He was waving that and muttering strange words. He turned to face her, his eyes frantic. "They're almost out! Blowing doesn't help. None of my wands will work either. This is bad. Really bad."

"Let me see," said Clover.

Oliver was right. The ashes weren't brighter. Just the opposite. All that remained of the glow was a single light in the center, like the final ember in a dying fire. Before, the ashes had radiated heat, but now they seemed cold. Clover reached out a finger and lightly touched the gray powder. For a moment, it seemed like another spark burst in the ash—or was it on her fingertip? She pulled back her hand. The spark went away, and the ember in the center flickered. Her heart quickened. She leaned down and gently blew on the ash.

Instead of glowing brighter, the ember flickered again . . . and a second later, it went out.

Only the ashes remained, gray and cold and lifeless.

"What have you done?!" cried Oliver.

"ME?! It wasn't me," Clover cried back.

"You're right," replied Oliver. "I should have figured this out by now. My brother would NEVER have let something like this happen. He'd have known right away what was going on. He'd have cured the sickness. I doubt Mr. Jams will let me stay here anymore. . . ."

"Who cares? It's the animals you should be worrying about. Don't you EVER think of the animals? What about Phoebe? What about HER?"

"I—I do care!" stammered Oliver. "I've been trying. . . ." He held up his wand.

"Everything was fine before you came here with

your books and wands and spells and relics. It's all your fault. *You* brought this sickness to the Agency." As she said it, Clover was sure it was true.

"I've only been trying to help," said Oliver. "But you don't want me to. You think you know everything!"

The pit of Clover's stomach felt full of fire, as though her heart had lodged itself there and was beating madly.

"*I* think *I* know everything? Me? It's YOU who's always saying what an EXPERT you are! Some expert! You're only an expert at . . . at . . . being an expert! You're annoying and stuck-up and *useless*! I wish . . . I wish you'd just leave!"

"Fine!" said Oliver. "I don't want to stay here anyway! Not with you!"

He gathered up his wands, pushed his glasses up his nose, and, just like that, stormed away.

10

Just Before Beyond

*G*ood riddance! thought Clover.

She didn't need Oliver. Dr. Nurtch was who she needed.

I'll get Gump to look after the Agency. He'll do a better job anyway.

After checking that the animals were safe and fed, Clover pocketed Dr. Nurtch's card. She could still hear Oliver upstairs in the tower, packing, but she didn't bother to say good-bye. There was nothing more to say. What mattered now was Phoebe and the rest of the animals.

Heading out, she almost tripped over Dipity.

Her kitten looked up at her and hissed.

"Dipity, it's just me," she said, bending down to pet him.

But he hissed again and bounded away.

Careful not to step on the pearls on the path (she'd have to sweep them up later), Clover stopped for a moment at the gate to let Gump know where she was going.

Gump stared past her stonily.

"I can't get Oliver to watch things because he's leaving."

Gump's expression didn't change.

"It's not my fault. He WANTS to leave."

Gump didn't even twitch.

"Just look after the Agency, okay? I'm counting on you."

As she closed the gate behind her, she glanced at Gump again. He still didn't blink. Not even once.

❋

The air was crisp, hinting at fall. In the Woods, twigs and grass crunched and crackled under Clover's feet, like a spitting fire. That was the only sound, however. Where were the birds, the squirrels, and the chipmunks? Was it her imagination, or were they avoiding her?

At last she reached the big tree at the crossroads.

The sign that read BEYOND pointed straight up, which was impossible, so she checked behind the tree and found a path—a twisty narrow one—that had to be the way. She started down it. Or really, "up" was the right word, because almost immediately the path began to ascend.

It was steep, zigzagging this way and that. Of course, she didn't want to go all the way to Beyond. She wanted to go "Just Before." How would she know when she'd reached it?

Soon she found out. The trees became smaller and more craggy the higher she hiked, and on one there was a sign.

GETTING CLOSER TO BEYOND, it read.

Oh good, Clover thought. She was so very hot.

She kept going until there were no trees at all, just rocks and moss.

Another sign, tacked to a boulder, let her know she was NEARLY AT BEYOND.

She paused to take some deep breaths, then headed

up, up, up some more, on a path that hugged the mountainside. *No wonder Dr. Nurtch needs Nanny*, thought Clover.

At last she came to the sign she was waiting for: JUST BEFORE BEYOND. It was on a post that stuck out from some rocks on the path.

She'd made it. But this was a cliff in the middle of nowhere. There was no hospital here! She sighed and slumped against the rock wall.

CREAK!

Clover jumped up. A large door in the side of the cliff had opened, and on the door, she saw something she had missed before. It was a tiny plaque that read: HILLSIDE HOSPITAL.

And beneath that: PLEASE WIPE DIRTY PAWS, CLAWS, OR HOOVES ON THE MAT PROVIDED.

Below the door there was a mat, gray like the stone under it.

Carefully, Clover pushed the door open wider and, after wiping her feet, stepped inside.

Instead of a small, dark cave, there was a large and luminous

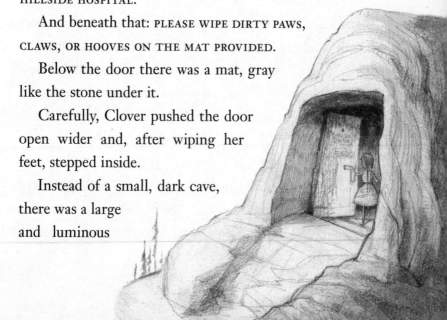

cavern, lit by what looked like giant glowworms hanging from the ceiling. Near the entrance was a stone bench with "Healthy Pet, Happy Vet" engraved on the backrest. A tiny table beside it was covered in pamphlets, much like the pamphlets at the Agency, except these were all to do with magical-animal wellness, like *Horn Health for Unicorns* and *Foods Scaly Animals Should Avoid*. In the center of the room was a much larger table, with vet's instruments displayed neatly on one end. Clover recognized the stethoscope and the magimeter, but the rest she didn't.

Although the tools looked interesting, what really caught Clover's attention were the animals.

The room echoed with chatters and cheeps, howls and honks. And no wonder. Circling the cavern were stalls and cages built right into the rock wall. Although

some were empty, most were filled. There were owls and bats and crows, some with casts on their legs, others whose feathers were unusual colors. One owl was cheeping like a swallow. There was a wart-free toad in a tank, and a magic kitten with a tail that looked like a puppy's, in a cage. In the biggest stall there was a horse—not just any horse, but a winged one with feathers like molten gold. One of its wings was bandaged.

And on the ground, under the examining table, was a creature that Clover didn't even know existed—a giant tortoise whose entire shell was covered in sparkling jewels. If it was hurt, its injury wasn't obvious. Clover couldn't see Nanny. Perhaps the goat was quarantined too.

"Dr. Nurtch?" Clover called out. "Dr. Nurtch, are you here?"

The vet didn't answer.

"Dr. Nurtch?"

From the back of the cave, Clover heard a cough, just like she had heard on the phone. She hurried toward the sound. "Dr. Nurtch?"

A door at the back of the room was partially open. More coughing came from behind it. Warily, Clover peeked around.

There, propped up on pillows on a stony bed, was Dr. Nurtch. At least, so Clover thought. It was hard to tell, because the vet had changed.

Dr. Nurtch was taller and her hair wasn't green, it was brown. Well, half of it. And instead of lumpy, her nose was straight. She didn't look like a troll anymore. She looked like a human. But when she saw Clover, her eyebrow raised in one piece, and Clover knew this was indeed the vet.

"Dr. Nurtch! Are . . . are you sick too?"

The vet opened her mouth as if to answer, but all that came out was more coughing. "Oh no!" cried Clover. "Dr. Nurtch, you can't be sick! I need your help. The Agency does. The animals are getting worse. Is there anything else we can try—maybe one of your moxtures?"

The vet shook her head feebly, then pointed at Clover with a trembling finger.

"Me? What do you want me to do?"

Dr. Nurtch just kept pointing, too weak to speak.

Maybe she isn't pointing at me, thought Clover. Behind her was the room filled with animals. "Oh! Are you worried about your patients? I'll make sure they're okay."

The vet gestured frantically, but this triggered another coughing fit.

"Just rest, Dr. Nurtch. I'll check on your animals. Then I'll go. I'll figure it out. I can do it. Just rest," she repeated, and hurried out of the room.

She checked the winged horse first. The horse still

had its wings, so that was a good sign. *If it was turning ordinary, it would be losing them, and its feathers*, thought Clover.

The winged horse snorted softly. "There, there," said Clover. "It's okay. I can take care of you if Dr. Nurtch can't." Clover gingerly reached out a hand to stroke its good wing.

The moment her fingers touched the golden feathers, something horrible happened. A spark leapt from her fingertips. The winged horse whinnied, and Clover stumbled backward. When she regained her balance, her eyes grew wide. The winged horse's feathers were drifting down like golden snow and melting before they reached the ground. As she watched, more and more feathers began to fall. The horse's wings were disappearing right in front of her eyes!

Clover gasped and backed away. *Thud!* Her foot hit something and she tripped. She reached out her hands to catch herself and her fingers brushed against the tortoise's shell. Instantly, emeralds and diamonds and rubies fell to the ground, just like the winged horse's feathers, and wisped away as if they were smoke.

The tortoise grunted softly and his black eyes, nearly buried by wrinkles, seemed to search her own.

Clover started to apologize, "I'm so very . . ." Then

she caught sight of something glowing. Something reflected in the tortoise's shiny shell.

She inched forward to see. It was her!

Her hair was shining with the sheen of a unicorn's mane, her freckles sparkling like the scales of a hippocampus, her eyes flashing with the fire of a phoenix. And her hands—her hands were *glowing*!

All at once she remembered . . . everyone commenting on her looks . . . the restless nights . . . touching Phoebe's ashes . . .

Dr. Nurtch hadn't been pointing at the animals.

Dr. Nurtch had been pointing at *her*.

She had touched all of the animals, even Nanny when she fetched the goat for Dr. Nurtch. And she'd shaken Dr. Nurtch's hand! And as for Oliver, there was that time that he'd bumped her while moving the fairy horses. . . .

Clover didn't know how or why, but SHE was the one making everyone ordinary. And just as they were turning ordinary, she was turning MAGIC!

She tried to remember when she had started feeling strange. Really, she hadn't felt like herself ever since . . . since she had gone to Oliver's room. *Since she had put on the necklace.*

She gasped and grabbed at the necklace, pulling the charm out from under her dress. It was glowing madly, just like her fingertips. Not in a pretty way. It was sinister, like a hot coal.

It wasn't just an abandoned necklace at the bottom of a box. It was a relic. A WICKED relic!

Clover tried to undo the clasp. But it was still stuck. She tried again—but it still wouldn't come. The metal was hot, whether from her fingers or from the clasp itself she wasn't sure. She twisted it around to have a look. The clasp wasn't just stuck—it was sealed shut.

There was no way to get the necklace off.

She began to panic, yanking and pulling at it. If she couldn't get the necklace off, she'd never be able to touch a magical animal again without draining its power. She'd ruined everything. She was cursed.

It was all her fault. If only she had left Oliver's things alone! As much as she was jealous of Oliver—yes, jealous, she could see that now—she didn't want to *be* Oliver. She wanted to be herself.

Sense not spells, *that* was her. She took a deep breath. *She* couldn't take the necklace off, but that didn't mean there wasn't a way.

She needed to get back to the Agency. "Now I understand, Dr. Nurtch!" she called, leaping to her feet. "I know what's causing the sickness. But don't worry, I'm going to get help!"

There was only one person who could help her. Only one person who might know what to do, because he was an expert in things like this.

She needed Oliver.

11
Clover's Curse

Clover raced back. Past "Nearly" and "Getting Closer," past the tree at the crossroads, along the path to the Agency. As she ran, she felt the necklace's heat building inside of her. Could they fix what the charm had done? Would the animals ever be themselves again? Would SHE ever be herself again?

"Please, please let Oliver be there," she whispered.

He wasn't in the front room or the small animals' room, or the stables. Clover raced upstairs, into his room. He wasn't there either.

Neither was his egg-shaped pillow or his egg-patterned blanket. The desk was cleared of books and papers and the wand-rack. Even the paperweight was gone. Oliver had left and taken everything with him. She was too late.

But if Oliver had taken everything, that meant his suitcase would be heavy. . . . And his wands weren't working, so he couldn't use magic. Maybe she could catch up to him? He couldn't have gotten far.

That's when she heard the barking.

Picnic was barking at something. It couldn't be a customer. She'd locked the front door behind her because of the quarantine. And it wasn't coming from the front room anyway. It was coming from the stables.

There were a million reasons Picnic might be barking. But somehow, Clover's heart knew exactly why. She raced down the stairs.

Oliver was sitting in the hay at the very back of the stables, with his suitcase beside him and his head in his

hands. Picnic barked again when he saw Clover, then turned back to Oliver and began to lick his face.

All at once, Clover felt a cool wash of relief.

"You're still here!"

Oliver didn't look up, only mumbled, "I was just leaving . . . out the back door."

"Oh no. Please don't!" said Clover.

"That's not what you said before."

"I—I know . . ." stammered Clover. "I . . . I was upset and, well, I . . . I wasn't myself." She pointed to the necklace, no longer hidden under her dress. The charm was still glowing madly. "Look, Oliver."

He didn't look up. He just mumbled, "I should go. I know I should. I might be a magical animal expert, but when it comes to actually working with magical animals, I'm an amateur. That's why I convinced Mr. Jams to let me stay here, so I could gain some practical experience. My brother has no problem working with animals. He, as my parents so often say, is a natural. Like you. But not me."

Clover couldn't believe it. "So . . . you aren't here to take over my job when summer ends?" she stammered.

"Take over? I can't even feed a unicorn." Oliver slumped even lower.

There was a long silence. Picnic whimpered and nudged Oliver's leg with his nose. Oliver didn't move. Clover shook her head. Oliver was jealous of *her*. She had no idea. All this time, she had been jealous of him!

"You're wrong," said Clover softly. "Plum loves your cinnamon-raisin oatmeal."

Oliver looked at her and smiled. His face was red and wet. "Really?"

"Yes." Clover cleared her throat. "But Plum isn't Plum anymore. None of the animals are themselves. And I'm not me either. Listen. I went to Dr. Nurtch's. I touched some animals. And I made them sick. Or at least, this thing did."

She held out the glowing charm.

Oliver's eyes went wide. "What IS that?"

"I . . . I don't know."

"Well, where did it come from?"

"Remember when you and Mr. Jams found me in your room? It was at the bottom of the box your brother sent you, and I took it."

"You took my relic?!" said Oliver.

"It was hidden at the bottom. I didn't think it was important. I thought it had been dropped in the box by accident." Clover paused. She took a deep breath.

"Still, I . . . I did take it. And I'm really sorry. . . ."

"Sorry?" Oliver peered at it more closely. "It's simply fascinating!"

"But, Oliver, it won't come off!"

"Oh!" said Oliver, his brow creasing.

"I think the clasp has sealed shut. And it's the reason the animals are all sick. What is it? Where is it from? What has it done? There must be a book somewhere that could tell us. . . ."

"I am sure there is," Oliver said. He pushed his glasses up his nose. "Now THAT I can take care of."

12

Moonbeams and Dragons

It didn't take long for Oliver to find an entry under "sun sprites" in *The Magical Animal Encyclopedia, Volume 4: Rare and Risky Animals*, while Clover sat on the couch, careful not to touch anything.

"Sun sprites are also known as 'monstrum solis,'" began Oliver. "They are a rare and elusive breed that utilizes a form of osmosis magic. . . ." He paused. "What I mean is, they feed off others' magic. They are born almost invisible and gather and crystalize sunbeams to make charms, like the one you're wearing. The charm collects magic and powers the sun sprite. See?"

He showed Clover the pictures beside the entry that showed a sun sprite's transformation.

One was a pixie, no bigger than a fingernail and dull as dust, the other a glowing orb, so bright it was impossible to make out its features, except for sharp teeth and pointed wings. It was wearing a charm around its neck that was bursting with sunbeams.

"Once they put on the charm, it's on them for life," continued Oliver.

"Oh no!" said Clover, fighting back the panic still in her heart. "How will we get it off? How will we give the magic back?"

It took Oliver a little longer, but eventually he managed to find an entry on how to remedy the sun sprite's effects too.

"There is a way," he said at last, "though I am not sure if we have what we need."

"What is it? Tell me!"

"You need to take a bath, in something very rare. Moonbeams. *Blue-moon* beams."

"Blue-moon beams!" exclaimed Clover. "Oh, Oliver, we do have some! Don't you remember? In the tack

125

room. You told me all about them when we . . . well, *I* . . . was making polish for the unicorns' horns."

"I *did*, didn't I?"

"Yes," said Clover, her voice full of smiles, "you did."

❂

There was only one bottle, but that was all they needed.

Oliver and Clover filled a big tub with warm water in the washing room and added a dash of the beams. They swirled silver and filled the room with the smells of a summer night.

Clover held her breath as she got in, with the necklace and her clothes still on. She'd never had a bath fully dressed before. But then, she'd never bathed in moonbeams either.

Would it work? She hoped more than anything it would. . . .

Immediately, the water began to swirl and spin and sizzle, the sound a spark makes when it is being doused. Oliver stepped back, and Clover watched in amazement as bubbles spilled out of the tub. Not just any kind of bubbles! Each bubble was shaped like a magical animal! There was a puppy bubble, and kitten bubbles, unicorn

bubbles . . . a whole parade of animals. Even a bubble shaped like a troll!

When a bubble popped, it burst into twinkles, like fireworks but without any sound. And the last one, the brightest, was red and gold and shaped like a bird, and when it popped, the last of the sizzling was over, and the water in the tub went completely still.

Clover felt still too. Her hands weren't tingling. Her face wasn't burning. She felt calm and cool. The blue-moon beams had worked!

She looked at the necklace. The sun charm—the wicked charm—was gone. It had dissolved completely away. All that was left was the chain, which undid easily and slipped right off her neck, falling with a plop into the water.

Oliver fetched her one of his robes to change into, and returned with a wand too. "Let's see if this works," he said. He waved the wand, and the robe folded into a neat square on the floor beside the tub. "My magic's back," he declared, grinning.

Clover grinned too, but she didn't want to encourage Oliver, so she shooed him out so she could get changed. Even in the wizard's outfit (which was sort of like a dress), she couldn't remember when she had last felt so normal, so good, so unmagical—so herself.

But what about the animals?

✿

The animals were back to normal, too. *Magical*-animal normal.

Dipity was green and Picnic was invisible. The magic kittens were zapping, floating, and tumbling. The fire salamanders were sizzling. The unicorns were prancing, showing off their milky-white horns (which, Clover noticed, looked remarkably sparkly, as though they had been polished!) and the tiny fairy horses were galloping around the stall. Thankfully, none of them had escaped, which they easily could have, right under the door slats. Clover and Oliver scooped them up and returned them to their cage. Neptune was big again and had his collar in his mouth, clearly wanting it to be put back around his neck. He was so smart!

"You can do it," Clover told Oliver. "He's really easy to manage." So Oliver climbed up the ladder and gestured to the hippocampus, who stayed perfectly still at the top of the tank while Oliver fumbled a few times but at last got the collar around the water-horse's neck.

Clover smiled, realizing she would be able to keep her promise after all when Meg came back the next day. And she'd have to phone Prudence and Humphrey too and let them know Picnic was better.

"But what about Phoebe?" she wondered aloud.

Clover and Oliver rushed to the rookery.

Clover's heart fell. The ash remained in the center of the sun, dull and gray. A shadow fell across the happiness of the afternoon.

"It's all my fault . . ." said Clover.

"It's not your fault," said Oliver. "It's mine. That necklace was here because of me. . . ."

Clover squeezed her eyes shut, trying hard not to cry.

But then they heard a cheep.

Oliver shook Clover's arm. "Look!"

Clover slowly opened her eyes—to the most marvelous sight.

From the gray ash, a tiny bird lifted its head. Her wings were red and gold like the sun, her tail like a flame, and her eyes like glowing coals.

Phoebe—baby Phoebe—was born!

"What should we do with it?" asked Clover, pointing to the chain, when they'd drained the water from the tub in the washing room.

"We could just throw it out," said Oliver. "It's not dangerous anymore. But I'd rather send it back to my brother. I'll write him a note. He really should be more careful about what he sends people. If he'd done his research properly, he would have known just how dangerous this relic was."

Clover agreed.

So, while Oliver packaged up the chain, Clover phoned Dr. Nurtch. This time, she got through at once and was so happy to hear the vet sounding gruff as usual. She was also happy to learn that Nanny, the winged horse, and the tortoise had all recovered as well. Dr. Nurtch described how she had woken up turning human. Even her voice had been changing and that's why she couldn't speak properly. "That's when I knew it wasn't a sickness. It was a curse, but I couldn't tell you when you visited."

"Well, I figured it out," said Clover. "Actually, Oliver and I did. We figured it out together."

"Together, did you?" said the vet. "Doesn't surprise me. Like I said, two heads are better than one."

"Oh," said Clover, remembering what the vet said when she left after her visit. "OH."

It actually *did* make sense after all.

Clover was about to go home—it was getting late now— when she remembered Gump.

Poor Gump!

She had touched him too. Had he lost his magic? Was he okay now?

"Sorry, Gump," said Clover. "Do you feel better?"

His mustache didn't move. Not even a little!

"Is he okay?" she asked Oliver.

"I'll find out," said Oliver. "Gluck gloo?" he said to the gnome.

"Glick, glog, glog," responded Gump.

"He says he's glad to see you're back to your usual self."

Clover couldn't believe it. "He talks!"

"Of course," said Oliver. "It's gnome language. Some gnomes speak English too, but not Gump. I studied it in my magical-animal courses. I was top of my class." For a moment Clover thought he was bragging, but then he added, "I could teach you."

"Really?" asked Clover, surprised.

Oliver nodded. "Of course. You know . . . there are lots of magical-animal correspondence courses. That's how I studied to become an expert. Perhaps you could take some courses too."

"But I'm not very good at school," said Clover.

"I can help you," said Oliver. "If you could teach me . . . you know, some practical animal basics . . . for myself, and even for my book. There needs to be a chapter on invisible-animal care. You could help me."

Clover nodded with all her might. "Of course!"

"I don't want to rely on my wands," Oliver continued.

"Well, actually," said Clover, her stomach grumbling, "I could use a bowl of that chicken noodle soup."

Oliver smiled. "Really?"

"Really," said Clover.

And so, after removing the quarantine sign, they sat on the steps of the Agency, in the cool evening air, and ate three bowls each of chicken noodle soup made by the Wellness wand. Phoebe rested on Oliver's shoulder, Dipity groomed his green fur by Clover's side, and Picnic's collar bobbed around as he chewed on the bone in the yard.

The soup was really tasty, with thick curly noodles, carrots, and parsley. Oliver produced the bottle of lemonade from Sabine too, and much to Clover's surprise the lemonade and soup went well together. Clover enjoyed every bit, as Oliver explained more about the magical-animal courses. Although, he told her, he still couldn't get his full Magical-Animal Doctorate without practical experience, he had finished all the courses long ago. As he described them to her, she grew more and more excited.

Could she really study magical animals? She *could* go to school, and work and study at the Agency afterward. Of course, she would miss playing with Emma in the

afternoons. But she could still be friends with Emma and work at the Agency, couldn't she? Just like Emma could make new friends at Pony Camp.

There was room in her life and her heart for lots. Just like there was room at the Agency. Lots of room for new animals and new friends—even slightly annoying ones.

Well, at least, *some* amount of room. Because just as she thought that, there was a *CRASH* and a *WHOOSH*, and then a holler, "Agency ahead!"

"What's that?" said Oliver, peering up.

"It sounded like Mr. Jams," said Clover.

It was indeed Mr. Jams.

And he was riding . . . a tree. No . . . it wasn't a tree. It was a dragon! The most incredible, extraordinary dragon Clover had ever seen. The scales covering its body were like leaves, its wings like branches draped with moss. Its long snout looked like a tree trunk.

Sir Windsmith was sitting behind Mr. Jams, and following them were four other dragons, all as strange and amazing as the first. They were varying shades of greens and browns, with tails like branches, crooked and twiggy.

"Forest dragons—a whole flight of them," whispered Oliver. "I've only read about forest dragons. I've never seen them before."

"Me neither," whispered Clover.

"So that was what their mission was about," said Oliver. "Forest dragons are some of the most prized creatures around. They live deep in the Woods, in families of four or five. They are very gentle and sometimes

become pets, but more often their heads become trophies. Sir Windsmith must have known these ones were in danger."

"And he and Mr. Jams rescued them," added Clover. "And brought them here."

The dragons landed on the lawn, near the bone. Clover could feel the wind from their wings and smell their smoke, like burnt pine needles. Sir Windsmith slipped off the dragon's back, and Mr. Jams followed with his suitcase. They looked tired and disheveled, but both were smiling broadly.

Phoebe swooped off Oliver's shoulder and landed on Sir Windsmith's. "Ah, there you are, my pet. You look wonderful—so youthful! I knew you would be safe here."

Clover gulped. She hoped Sir Windsmith wouldn't be too upset when he learned what had actually happened. She and Oliver would have to tell him later—if they could get a word in edgewise. Sir Windsmith was still going on. "How I missed you—enough, yes, to warrant a rhyme!

A knight is not right
with his pet far from sight.

Or maybe—"

Phoebe squawked.

"Blithering bones, Walter. One more rhyme, and I swear!" said Mr. Jams, but there was a twinkle in his eye.

He turned to Clover and Oliver. "We need your help to ready the stables. All the big stalls will be needed, with proper precautions for fire and smoke. Can you do it?"

"Of course!" Clover and Oliver burst out at the same time.

Clover looked at Oliver and smiled. He smiled back.

This was the Agency, and anything was possible—as long as the door was open and your heart was too.

ACKNOWLEDGMENTS

I firmly believe, as Dr. Nurtch says, that "two heads are better than one," especially when it comes to creating a book. In fact, the more heads the better, and I am so grateful for all the smart, thoughtful, amazing people that helped me with this story. To my friends, especially my writing group, the Inkslingers, and my teaching partner, Lee Edward Fodi. To my family, including my mom and dad and especially my brother, who is a nurse, and his girlfriend, who is a marine biologist and helped me with all my funny vet questions, like how to care for a hippocampi. To everyone at Disney Hyperion and HarperCollins Canada, especially my fantastic editors, Rotem Moscovich and Hadley Dyer, and assistant editor, Julie Moody. To Alexandra Boiger, whose beautiful illustrations always give me a thrill. Particular thanks to my incredible agent, Emily Van Beek; my dear husband, Luke, my writing soul mate; Vikki Vansickle; and my friend and poet Tiffany Stone, who helped SO much with plotting and editing this book, and knows Clover just about as well as I do.